DESTINY'S CHASE

A novella by
VANESSA FRANK

DESTINY'S CHASE
by Vanessa Frank

All Scripture quotations, in this publication are from the HOLY BIBLE, NEW INTERNATIONAL VERSION ® NIV ® Copyright © 1973, 1978, 1984, 2011 by Biblica, Inc.TM. All rights reserved worldwide.

"Nothing I Can Do About It Now" lyrics written by Beth Nielsen Chapman.

ISBN 978-0985694104

Cover Illustration: Lady Symphonia
Back Cover Design: Sarah Pharo
Author Photographs: Amy Harris

First Edition 2012

I dedicate this book to Yeshua. This book will always remain
first and foremost
my love letter to you.

and

To my parents, for first giving me life, and then introducing me
to the source of life. *"Blessed is the one who perseveres under trial
because, having stood the test, that person will receive the crown of life that
the Lord has promised to those who love him."* (James 1:12)

Chapters

Prologue...1

1. My Little Girl...3

2. Never Wanted Nothin' More.....................11

3. Ring Of Fire...21

4. I Walk The Line.......................................29

5. Inside Your Heaven................................35

6. When I Get Where I'm Going..................41

7. Picture To Burn.......................................49

8. Your Cheatin' Heart................................55

9. She Wouldn't Be Gone...........................63

10. The House That Built Me........................71

11. Always On My Mind................................75

12. Here Comes Goodbye...........................79

13. The Dance...85

God demonstrates his own love for us in this:
While we were still sinners, Christ died for us.

Romans 5:8

For he chose us in him before the creation of the world to be holy and blameless
in his sight.

Ephesians 1:4

For those God foreknew he also predestined to be conformed to the image of his Son,
that he might be the firstborn among many brothers and sisters. And those he
predestined, he also called; those he called, he also justified; those he justified, he also
glorified.

Romans 8:29-30

I bathed you with water and washed the blood from you and put ointments on you. I
clothed you with an embroidered dress and put sandals of fine leather on you. I
dressed you in fine linen and covered you with costly garments. I adorned you with
jewelry: I put bracelets on your arms and a necklace around your neck, and I put a
ring on your nose, earrings on your ears and a beautiful crown on your head. So you
were adorned with gold and silver; your clothes were of fine linen and costly fabric
and embroidered cloth. Your food was honey, olive oil and the finest flour. You
became very beautiful and rose to be a queen. And your fame spread among the
nations on account of your beauty, because the splendor I had given you made your
beauty perfect, declares the Sovereign Lord.

Ezekiel 16:9-14

Prologue

This is a tale of two different worlds, two different eras, two different lives. It is the story of a love that overcomes the confines of time, and reaches into depths of eternity. It is the story of ancient days in the Middle East, and of modern day America. It is the story of one man, and one woman…

Chapter One

MY LITTLE GIRL

The glass cut through her skin like a knife through butter. She barely registered the pain, as the dark torment that raged in her soul was so much more agonizing than any physical sensation ever could be. As she cut deeper a memory from the distant past briefly flitted through her mind. For a moment she remembered innocence. For a moment she remembered joy. For a moment she remembered love. But then as soon as the memory had come, it left. And all that remained was this ever present, all consuming darkness that enveloped her mind, body, and soul.

But soon it would be over. Soon she would be released from this pain. Soon she would be free.

Five year old Destiny Morgan thumbed through a dusty box of her father's old 12–inch records. She loved everything about them: the slightly musty smell of the covers, the sound that the disc made as it slid out of the package, the glitzy clothes and bouffant hair of the women in the photos. But more than anything she loved the sound that would come from her father's record player when he'd put on whichever album she'd chosen: country music – the sound of her secret universe.

She'd struggle to choose between albums – every one of them told a tale that made her mind come alive with story and color. But more often that not her father and her would end up spending some part of their lazy afternoons together listening to "Nothing I Can Do About It Now" by Willie Nelson. Sequestered in the basement, enjoying a world of their own, Destiny would stand on his desk chair and emphatically sing along:

"I've got a long list of real good reasons for all the things I've done. I've got a picture in the back of my mind of what I've lost and what I've won."

Destiny loved to sing, and indeed she could not remember a time when that hadn't been the case. Since before she could even speak her father would sing to her as he'd strum his old 1969 Guild Starfire VI guitar. She had barely started forming words before he was teaching her his favorite old country standards. Patsy Cline, Johnny Cash and The Judds were all her childhood companions, but no more so than Willie Nelson, whom she had taken an instant liking to the day after her fourth birthday.

Sometimes her father would allow her to pick up his Guild Starfire and would show her how to wrap her tiny hands across the ebony fretboard to pick out certain sounds. The strings hurt her fingers and so when he would invite her to play the guitar her interest would vary between a reluctant shaking of her head to wild enthusiasm. As her father never knew which mood to anticipate he'd simply ask her and then laugh with amusement at her reaction.

But even when she didn't want to play the guitar Destiny just loved to sit in her father's lap. She loved the feeling of being hugged between the guitar and him, the embrace of his strong arms wrapped around her as he played, and the warmth of his breath on the top of her head as he sang. There was always a space on his lap for Destiny, and she knew that she had only to ask. Sometimes she didn't even have to say the words – her father would take one look at her, scoop her up in his arms, pick up his guitar and ask her what song she wanted to sing.

For the last couple of years Destiny had participated in junior talent competitions. She would rarely win, but that didn't matter to her – she just enjoyed being on stage and knowing that her Daddy was watching. They would carefully rehearse in the basement for weeks beforehand, with her father giving her instructions as to how to stand, how to breathe and how to use the inflections of her voice to convey a particular sentiment. He would patiently spend hours rehearsing the same song over and over again, continuing to tirelessly offer up rapturous encouragement after each and every performance.

Destiny always felt safe when they rehearsed in the basement, tucked away from a world that she didn't always understand. She didn't have siblings to play with, and her parents were continually at war. Though they would rarely raise their voices, her mother would speak in a certain tone, a cold and menacing tone, which would usually be followed by an angry and frustrated response from her father. Sometimes he wouldn't say anything at all, but Destiny knew that his eyes were saying a thousand words. Most nights she would fall asleep listening to the muted sound of arguing coming from downstairs. At times the tension would become unbearable, and so Destiny would curl up in her bed and wish that she could just escape to a different world, a world far away.

Then one day this all came to an abrupt end. Destiny was woken early in the morning by the sound of yelling emanating from her parents' bedroom. As she crawled out of bed bleary–eyed she knew that this argument was like no other. Fear gripped hold of her as she placed her hand on the handle of her bedroom door. For some reason she knew that as soon as she opened that door there would be no going back. She took a deep breath, and pulled the latch.

As she walked into her parents' bedroom she saw her father stood with his back to her as her mother yelled obscenities at him. A duffel bag lay on the bed, which appeared to have been quickly stuffed with a few items of clothes.

"Daddy?" Destiny asked in a voice that was almost a whisper. He immediately spun round to look at her. She did not understand the look on his face, but she knew it was not good.

"What's going on?" she asked, her bottom lip starting to quiver. When he saw this his jaw clenched, and he got down on his knees in front of her so that he was at her height.

"Destiny, I'm…I'm going to have to go away for a while. But it's just for a short while, and then you and I are going to be together."

Destiny suddenly felt as though she couldn't breath as darkness suddenly closed in on her.

"Is it because of me Daddy?"

Her father's face crumpled as a tear started to slowly tumble down his cheeks. His voice broke as he spoke.

"No, Destiny it's not because of you. I love you so much. It's just…it's just that I'm going to go stay with Uncle Pete for a while."

"Will you come to my competition next week?"

"Of course baby, I'll be there."

And with that he swept her up into his arms. She could feel the back of her pajamas grow wet with his tears as he held her tight. She held onto him as though she was holding onto life itself.

Eventually he released her, but she continued to cling to him, aware that the moment she let go he was going to leave. Lovingly, he prised himself away from her, picked up the duffel bag and quickly walked to the front door.

"No Daddy, don't leave, don't leave, please don't leave! I'll do anything you want!" she begged.

He turned back to look at her. He tried to speak, but then tears overcame him and so he simply tried to smile. He turned to open the door, and then was gone.

As the door slammed shut, Destiny felt sure her world had just ended.

She collapsed on the ground, sobbing. Her Mom grabbed her harshly by the arm, and dragged her to her bedroom.

"Shut up!" she yelled. "I can't deal with a scene from you right now!" She slammed the door shut.

Destiny climbed into her bed, and pulled the covers over her head. Darkness. Nothingness. Right now, that's all she wanted.

The next week Destiny stood on stage at the 5th Annual Junior Sing competition. As she sang "Love Can Build A Bridge" she scanned the sea of faces avidly, looking for her Dad. She desperately wanted him. But he was nowhere to be found.

She finished her performance and walked off the stage. A tidal wave of grief and disappointment hit her, and she felt as though she was going to drown in it.

It was a whole month until Destiny saw her father next. The meeting was tense and awkward. She asked him questions about when he was going to come home, but he didn't have answers. She got upset, and he couldn't say anything to comfort her.

After that the visits became further and further apart. And then one day they ceased entirely.

And, bit by bit, Destiny stopped singing.

Yeshua was just eight days old the first time his parents took him to the temple in Yerushalayim. As his mother, Miryam, carried him in her arms through the court an old man called Shim'on, who was righteous and devout, ran up to her and placed his hand on her shoulder. When she swung round she found herself looking up at eyes that were full of wisdom and truth.

"My name is Shim'on", he told her "and I knew I was to come here today. I have been praying for many years for our land to be healed, and I heard a voice telling me that I would not die before I laid eyes on the one that would be our Savior." He pointed to Yeshua, "This is him, is it not?" he asked.

His mother was deeply moved, as Shim'on had voiced the truth she kept buried deep in the confines of her heart, a cherished secret, that her son had a supernatural power and purpose. Without saying a word she nodded her head.

"Would you like to hold him?" she asked gently. "His name is Yeshua."

Shim'on nodded, with a look in his eye of one who knows he has just met his destiny.

As Shim'on took Yeshua in his arms he looked up at the sky in sheer awe and exclaimed "Adonai, as you have promised, you may now dismiss your servant in peace! For my eyes have seen your salvation, which you have prepared in the sight of all nations: a light for revelation to the Gentiles, and the glory of your people Isra'el!"

Yeshua's father and mother marveled at Shim'on's words.

"May the Father bless you both!" Shim'on declared, looking at them. Then he looked Miryam straight in the eyes and confided in a warning tone, "This child is destined to cause the falling and rising of many in Isra'el, and to be a sign that will be spoken against, so that the thoughts of many hearts will be revealed. And a sword will pierce your own soul too."

Before she could respond an old prophet by the name of Hannah Bat-P' nu' el interrupted them at that very moment. Hannah Bat-P' nu' el had been a widow most of her life and almost never left the temple, but worshiped night and day, fasting and praying. And as she saw Shim'on holding Yeshua she started exclaiming to all around "Praise be to Adonai! Praise be our maker! For he has brought us the one who is going to redeem us! The one who is going to deliver us! Our Savior!"

Yeshua's parents simply cherished and marveled at all these promises.

Every year Yeshua's family would travel to Yerushalayim for the festival of Pesach. The year he was twelve years old they went to the festival, as custom required.

After the festival was over the family started on their journey home. But Yeshua didn't go with them; he stayed behind, without their knowledge. Supposing he was somewhere in the caravan, they traveled on for a full day. But then as the hours passed on, they did not see him, so they started to worry. They began looking for him among their relatives and friends. When they did not find him they hurriedly traveled back to Yerushalayim to find him.

For three whole days they searched high and low, his mother growing increasingly anxious with every passing moment. On the third day they finally happened upon him in the temple courts. He was sitting amongst the teachers, deeply engrossed in what they were saying and asking them all sorts of questions. Scholars young and old surrounded him, shooting questions back at him and marveling between themselves at his wisdom. They looked amazed at the answers he gave.

When his parents saw this scene, they were astonished. His mother ran up to him, grabbed him and exclaimed, "Son, why have you treated us like this? Your father and I have been anxiously searching for you!"

"Why were you searching for me?" he exclaimed with genuine surprise. "Didn't you know I had to be in my father's house?"

His parents did not understand what he was saying to them. "Come, we need to go home!" his mother declared, thoroughly bewildered and exhausted.

So Yeshua stood up to leave.

"Your destiny is with us, master!" a voice called out. Yeshua turned round and saw that it came from an old teacher sat in the corner. He noticed that the man was blind.

"You see well," Yeshua said. And with that he left them, and joined his parents on the journey back home.

It was not long after this that Yeshua's family celebrated his coming of age with him. As his father gave him a tallit, a prayer shawl, he told him "Son, when you place this over your head you can speak to God, and he will hear you."

So that night, in the darkness of the night, Yeshua placed the tallit over his head, and prayed to God.

And as he did so he heard a voice speaking back to him. It sounded like thunder.

Chapter Two

NEVER WANTED NOTHIN' MORE

Destiny could feel the blood pumping through her veins in anger. Though she was now eighteen, she felt like her mom treated her like she was still a child.

"I am so fed up of doing everything for you!" her mother yelled. "You never do anything around here!"

"Nothing I do is ever good enough for you!" Destiny screamed back, and picked up the car keys.

"What, you're going to leave?" her mother taunted. "Oh, don't worry about me – I'll just finish cleaning up after you!"

Destiny just rolled her eyes and turned to leave, but then she heard her mother murmur under her breath, "You're just like your Father."

She immediately froze, and then whirled round to glare at her mother. "What did you say?" she demanded in a low but threatening tone.

"Nothing," her mother said with pursed lips.

"Oh, yes you did!" Destiny snarled.

"Ok, fine, I said that you are just like your father!" her mother said in a spiteful tone. "You're selfish and you're a loser, just like him!"

Pure hatred filled Destiny's mind as rage swept through her like a fire. "I might be a loser like my father but at least I'm not anything like you!" she screamed.

Before she even had time to see the look on her mother's face she walked out the door, slamming it behind her.

By the time Destiny entered the bar hatred was consuming her
every thought. She barely registered greeting her friends or ordering the
first of many drinks. She knocked back a double shot of vodka
purchased with her trusty fake ID followed by rum and coke and
whatever else was on offer. It soon all blended into a blur of false
laughter and inebriation as she battled to douse with liquor the fire of
anger that burned in her heart.

As the night went on she increasingly felt good about herself
once more. However, this haze of numb bliss was suddenly abruptly
pierced by a bookish young woman who was doing her best Leann
Rimes on the karaoke machine, but failing to please all but a few of the
most inebriated patrons.

Destiny snorted at her and looked at her friends. "Kill me
now," she said derisively.

"I'd like to see you do better" her friend Jayden ribbed.

"I don't sing." Destiny quickly retorted.

"So you're afraid," Jayden taunted.

"No I'm not, I just don't sing," she said, a little defensively.

"You're chicken."

"No, I'm not!" she said aggressively. "You take that back!"

"Prove me wrong," he exclaimed drunkenly with a teasing
smile on his face.

Fury welled up in Destiny. "Fine!" she spat at him.

She stormed across the bar, over to the karaoke machine and
wrenched the microphone out of the hands of the totally unsuspecting
woman, bringing her rendering of Leann Rimes to a screeching halt.
The entire bar went silent.

"Play 'Nothing I Can Do About It Now'!" Destiny ordered the
karaoke machine operator, who simply stood there gawking at her in
shock.

"Play 'Nothing I Can Do About It Now'!" Destiny shouted at
him once more, abruptly awakening him out of his stupor.

The woman who had been singing started protesting loudly,
but Destiny simply pushed her out of the way as the first few chords of
"Nothing I Can Do About It Now" began to play.

"I've got a long list of real good reasons for all the things I've done," she
sang as she moved in a seductive but somewhat drunken manner.

*"I've got a picture in the back of my mind of what I've lost and what I've
won."* The bar started to cheer her on, as men threw somewhat crude
encouragements her way.

"I've survived every situation." Destiny kicked a chair against the bar. Without missing a single word she climbed up onto it so that all could see her.

"Knowing when to freeze and when to run." She careened wildly, whipping her long hair around between lyrics.

"And regret is just a memory written on my brow and there's nothing I can do about it now." She moved and rolled her body to the music, as men hollered words of encouragement and women laughed drunkenly.

Destiny continued the song until the end, and as the music died down Destiny took a wild bow to her audience as people applauded and whistled. She got down off the bar, almost falling off as she did so, handed the microphone to a stranger and staggered back over to her friends.

"So, who were you calling chicken?"   she asked Jayden pointedly.

"Well, for someone who doesn't sing, you sure have a set of pipes on you!"

"I think you owe me a drink. And you know what else I think, I think…"

At that very moment a man pushed his way abruptly into their group. He looked to be in his early thirties, and he had a strong dominating presence. He stared at Destiny straight in the eyes.

"You were amazing," he declared.

"Who is this jerk?" Jayden retorted.

"Rick McKenzie from Elite Entertainment", he replied, without taking his eyes off of Destiny for a single moment. He reached into his pocket and held out a business card. "I'm a talent scout, and I'd like to speak to you about your future."

"I don't have a future. Rick McKenzie from Elite Entertainment," she informed him curtly, and then turned back to look at Jayden. "As I was saying, I think…"

"Really, I must insist," Rick McKenzie interjected. "I think you do."

Destiny turned to glare at him. "And I suppose you're here to make all my dreams come true?" she asked mockingly. "Are you my fairy godmother? Are you going to turn a pumpkin into a carriage for me?"

Destiny's friends all laughed raucously at her mockery.

"You need to take my card," he insisted unfazed. He held it towards her again.

She gave him a critical look and stared at him intimidatingly. He stared right back at her, refusing to back down. Finally she rolled her eyes and grabbed the card.

"Fine, Mr. Fancy Pants, I'll take your blessed card," she said derisively.

"I look forward to hearing from you" he declared assertively, and then departed without a further word.

A few days passed, with Destiny and her mother living in an ice-cold silence of noisy contempt. Then one day, as Destiny was lying on her bed texting a friend, her mom abruptly opened her bedroom door.

"Destiny, did you take the garbage out last night?" she asked, with a look on her face that suggested she already knew the answer to her question.

Destiny suddenly realized she'd completely forgotten about her weekly chore. "Erm…I guess I forgot," she said dismissively.

"Destiny you know the trash is only collected once a week!" her mom exclaimed.

"I know alright! It's not like we're going to die if the trash isn't collected," Destiny retorted while continuing to text.

"You know, I ask you to do one lousy thing all week long, and you can't even do that! It's always the same thing, I have to do everything myself, and you just expect me to look after you like you're royalty or something. Well I have news for you princess; if you don't pull your act together you're going to spend the rest of your life being good for nothing! And no man is ever going to want you!"

"What, like you?" Destiny responded contemptuously.

"I think you'll find I know a thing or two about the way life works. And if you think you're going to get anywhere in life with that kind of an attitude you're absolutely wrong!"

"Well, actually there is someone who thinks I'm amazing," Destiny said with attitude.

"Who, Jesus?" her mom mocked.

"No," Destiny retorted with disdain. "A talent scout. A good talent scout. He saw me sing and told me he thinks I'm incredible."

"Oh yeah, right. I'm sure he's a real class act."

"Actually he is, thank you very much."

"And where did you meet this 'talent scout'?"

"That's none of your business."

"Destiny, stop being a silly little girl! He's probably just some loser who is trying to get into your pants. I bet he says that to all the girls, and you're probably the only one who is stupid enough to actually fall for it."

"What do you know? What do you know about anything?! You're just some stupid, bitter, old woman who hates everyone!"

"Well, any mother who has to live with such a disappointment of a daughter would understand why I feel permanently drained!"

"You know what, I'm going to get a record deal, and I'm going to make a ton of money, and then I'm going to move out. And then, you know what I'm going to do, Mother? I'm going to chose to never, ever see you again!"

"Fine!" her mother barked back, and stormed out of the room.

Destiny, seething with anger, rolled off the bed and stalked over to her closet. She threw the door open violently and pulled out her handbag. She ripped it open and turned it over, allowing all the contents to fall on the floor in a pile. She quickly rummaged through the items on the floor.

"Where is it? Where is it?" she muttered to herself.

She shook the bag, but nothing more came out, and so she growled in frustration. Then she looked in the bag. There, stuck in the lining, was the card.

"There!" she declared with a self–satisfied smirk.

She picked up her cell phone, and quickly punched in the number on the card.

"Hello? Is this Elite Entertainment? Can I please speak to Rick McKenzie?"

The agency reception was more intimidating than she'd imagined. The marble floor was so shiny she could practically see her reflection in it, and the reception desk was an impressive concoction of mahogany and frosted glass, with an equally polished and perfectly coiffed receptionist behind it. The agency's logo was projected onto the wall, and the many glistening plaques that surrounded it implied a level of success that Destiny hadn't quite anticipated. She was just considering picking up one of the meticulously arranged magazines when Rick brusquely walked into the room.

"Destiny, good to see you again," he said with a broad smile. Thanks for coming to meet us."

"Yeah, sure," she said as she stood up.

"Do you have two songs prepared like I asked you to?"

"Yeah," she said nervously.

"Good, so I'm going to take you in to see Bob Bailey. He's the top guy here, and he's keen to see you for himself. So it's very important that you do your best, okay?"

"Okay," she said, a little unsure of what to think.

Rick smiled at her. "Okay then. It's this way."

He led her out into a long corridor. As they walked down it Destiny lost count of how many framed records she passed. Eventually they reached a large meeting room. A rather overweight man in his fifties sat behind the table, busily checking his phone.

"Bob, this is Destiny."

The man glanced up.

"So, Destiny. I've heard a lot about you. Are you going to impress me today?" he asked.

"I don't know," she said a little defensively. He raised his eyebrows and shot a pointed look at Rick. She suddenly realized that this was not the response he was expecting to hear.

"I mean, yeah, yeah I will," she quickly countered.

"Right then," he said with a hint of skepticism. "You may proceed."

"What, you mean, like, now?" she asked.

"Yes, like now."

"Erm, okay." She coughed loudly to clear her throat.

She launched into her first song, staring at the wall above Bob Bailey's head in a vein attempt to offset the nerves that she was suddenly experiencing. As she sang she was vividly aware of the intensity with which both men were staring at her, and she could feel herself speeding up the lyrics as the pressure started getting to her. She glanced down briefly at Bob Bailey, and saw that he was taking notes. This only made her more nervous. Eventually she completed the song. There was an uncomfortable silence.

"Destiny, would you do me a favor?" Bob asked. "For the next song I want you to look right at me while you're singing. I want you to take your time and sing it like you were singing it to me, understood?"

"Yes, sir," she answered nervously.

She started to sing the next song, and as she did so she felt increasingly confident. She could feel all the lessons her father had given her coming back to her mind.

When she finished there was silence again. She had absolutely no idea whether they'd loved her performance or absolutely hated it.

Bob put down his pen and stared at her intently.

"Destiny, I'm going to do something I very rarely do. I'm going to make you an offer right here and now that we at Elite Entertainment would like to formally represent you as one of our artists. You have a very unique sound, and there's a quality to your voice that makes you an absolutely perfect fit for country. Rick can sit down with you and tell you in detail what we can offer. But if you're serious about making a career as a country singer, I think you'll find that there is no one who can open doors for you than we at Elite Entertainment can."

Destiny's heart started racing. Surely, this was the beginning of something good.

Destiny rummaged through the boxes that had accumulated over the years in the basement. As she did so her fingers left traces in the thick layer of dust that had settled on them. Indeed it had been years since she'd spent this much time down there – the room was entirely too full of memories that she would much rather forget.

Suddenly she happened upon it: her father's old Guild Starfire. She carefully picked it up and set it down on her lap. She lovingly gazed at the ebony fretboard, the pearl inlays, the Guild-branded tailpiece. It was beautiful.

She gently strummed her fingers across the strings. They would need to be replaced. But it was perfect for her.

In the guitar store the clerk was only too happy to help her with the Guild Starfire.

"I ain't seen one of these in a long time!" he exclaimed as he carefully admired its beautiful craftsmanship. "All it needs is some new strings and it'll play like pure magic," he declared as he proceeded to loosen the tuning keys and cut the old strings with a wire cutter.

Destiny watched as he pulled the strings out and then gently cleaned the fretboard with a soft cloth.

"Can I put on the new strings?" she asked.

"Sure," he said as he ripped open a pack. "It's very simple, you just do this," he said, and proceeded to show her how.

Destiny carefully listened to his instructions, and then under his supervision she proceeded to restring all the rest. She tightened them all just right, until the very last one was done.

She picked up the guitar and held it up to admire her handiwork. Her father would be proud.

⅒❦⅒❦⅒❦⅒

Yeshua's cousin was a prophet by the name of Yochanan Ben-Z'kharyah. He was as strong and uncompromising of a man as one could possibly hope for. Of late he had been living in the arid wilderness of Y'hudah, preaching to all who would listen about the need for a baptism of repentance for the forgiveness of sins, and boldly declaring to them, "Repent, for the kingdom of heaven has come near!"

Yochanan wore clothing made of camel's hair, with a leather belt wrapped around his waist. He lived off of locusts and wild honey. Many said that he was mad, but vast crowds would still travel from all of Y'hudah and indeed the whole of the Yarden region to hear what he had to say. Many of them were swayed by the power of his words and the intensity of his passion, and chose to confess their sins and partake of this new ritual. So he spent his days preaching to many, and baptizing them one by one in the river.

One day some of the religious leaders of the region joined the assembled crowds. Upon seeing them a great anger filled him, and he pointed his finger at them and yelled "You brood of vipers! Who warned you to flee from the coming wrath? Produce fruit in keeping with repentance! And do not think you can say to yourselves, 'We have Avraham as our father.' I tell you that out of these stones God can raise up children for Avraham! The axe is already at the root of the trees, and every tree that does not produce good fruit will be cut down and thrown into the fire!"

The crowd turned to look at the religious leaders to see their response. But they said nothing, and simply glared at Yochanan with intense hatred. Then they turned their backs to him, and left with a haughty look of disdain on their faces.

Yochanan knew in that moment that he had just further worsened his bad relationship with the local religious community, who already spoke of him with disparaging and callous remarks. These religious leaders knew all too well that the people were waiting for confirmation of what they were wondering in their hearts — whether Yochanan might possibly be the Savior that had been prophesied to them. They abhorred him for the power this gave him.

Yochanan turned his mind from these thoughts and returned to addressing the crowd.

"I baptize you with water for repentance," he declared. "But after me comes one who is more powerful than I, whose sandals I am not worthy to carry! He will baptize you with the Holy Spirit and fire! His winnowing fork is in his hand, and he will clear his threshing floor, gathering his wheat into the barn and burning up the chaff with unquenchable fire!"

As soon as he was finished speaking, the sound of whispering and murmuring shot through the crowd as people debated what he had just said. But Yochanan did not care, for he did not value the opinion of men.

When the very next day Yochanan saw Yeshua coming toward him his heart started to race.

He immediately stopped what he was doing and turned to address the large crowd that was assembled. "This is the one I meant when I said a man who comes after me has surpassed me because he was before me! I myself did not know him, but the reason I came baptizing with water was that he might be revealed to us! I saw the spirit come down from heaven as a dove and remain on him. And I myself did not know him, but the one who sent me to baptize with water told me the man on whom you see the Spirit come down and remain is the one who will baptize with the Holy Spirit!"

Yeshua walked right up to Yochanan and smiled warmly. "Yochanan, will you baptize me?" he asked.

"But I need to be baptized by you!" Yochanan exclaimed.

Yeshua simply placed his hand on Yochanan's shoulder and told him in a reassuring tone, "Let it be so now, it is proper for us to do this to fulfill all righteousness."

Yochanan hesitated. But as he looked into Yeshua's eyes he knew what the right thing was to do. So, trembling, Yochanan led Yeshua down to the water and they waded in until they were waist deep. Yochanan stood by his side, and then with all his strength dunked him deep into the muddy, green water.

For a moment Yeshua disappeared from Yochanan's view as he submerged under the water's surface. Then Yochanan pulled Yeshua back up out of the water. At that very moment a rapturous sound came from the sky above. Yochanan and all those in the assembled looked up. There they saw a beautiful light descending rapidly towards Yeshua. It looked like a dove, but its colors and shades were entirely supernatural. It alighted on him with a mystical power.

Then a voice from heaven loudly declared, "This is my son, whom I love. With him I am well pleased!"

The crowd gasped in awe, some of them dropping to their knees, while others turned to flee, as some simply stood there watching with their mouths gaping open.

Yeshua calmly made his way to the riverbank. A silent reverence fell upon the crowd as he started on his journey home.

Chapter Three

RING OF FIRE

Rick was wise in a way that Destiny had never encountered before. He always knew how to direct conversations exactly where he wanted them to go, and he handled each and every situation with calm assertiveness. From conference rooms to industry parties, he was always working a room somewhere. When she was in his presence his confidence and authority made her feel safe, a feeling she hadn't experienced in a long time.

So when Rick first started speaking to her flirtatiously she thought she had to be imagining it. She could not envisage that a man of such stature would be interested in her. He always seemed to have women at his beck and call, and she knew that more than one of them had been intimately involved with him. While most men were needy and desperate around her, and she'd long since learned how to manipulate them, Rick was absolutely immovable. But rather than being frustrated by his resistance to her charms, she grew in admiration for his unwavering composure and strength.

So when the odd flirtatious undertone, the odd brief glance of the eyes would occur in their interactions, she dismissed her interpretation of it as unlikely. But over time as Rick's flirtations became more and more overt she found herself liking the commanding assertion that he spoke to her with.

But then every time Destiny thought he was going to make a move he would suddenly start acting indifferent, and as this back and forth persisted she found herself increasingly wanting to please him. To her shock when she'd be rewarded from time to time with a lingering gaze or a playful comment she'd find herself instantly responding with uncharacteristic enthusiasm. But then he'd quickly push her away, and she'd find herself both hating herself for being so needy, and wanting him all the more.

This game went on for weeks. With every passing week, and every rebuffed advance, Destiny found herself feeling increasingly frustrated and enamored with this strong man who always seemed to know the right thing to say in every situation.

⤮

Destiny stood alone on the balcony. She'd never been to a penthouse before, but as she looked at the sea of lights below she could see why people coveted them. A sea of lights spread out below her, and she felt as though she was on top of the world.

The sound of gossiping and clinking of glasses drifted out from the apartment behind her. From what Rick had told her most of Nashville's music industry were assembled there. As much as she knew that he'd be wanting her to work the room, she needed a minute to just be alone. All this whirlwind of activity was starting to overwhelm her and she needed a moment to just breathe.

As she inhaled the cold November air she heard the sound of the balcony door opening as someone stepped out onto the balcony. A moment later she felt a warm, masculine hand caress the small of her back, which her backless dress left exposed.

"You mustn't get cold," Rick whispered in her ear.

"What does it matter to you?" she retorted.

He leaned back against the balcony rail and took a sip of his whisky. "You're angry," he observed with a wry smile.

"No, I'm not," she responded, a little too fast to be in any way convincing.

"You're grasping that balcony rail so tight I'm a little worried you're going to bend the metal," he remarked with amusement.

She looked away from him. "What do you know?" she said with thinly veiled anger.

He chuckled. "More than you think," he said.

"Oh yeah, like what, Mr. Fancy Pants?" she snapped.

"Well, I know that you are going to be very, very famous one day," he said.

"Tell me something I don't know," with a slight roll of her eyes.

"And I know that you and I are going to dominate this industry together," he continued.

"Well, that's just great," she said curtly.

"And I know that you have absolutely no idea of the effect you have on me."

Destiny was just opening her mouth to say something derogatory, when his words suddenly sunk in. She shut her mouth and spun round to look at him.

"I...eh....what?" she not so eloquently gasped.

He laughed, took a sip of his whisky, and placed the glass on the balustrade. Then with a knowing smile he pulled Destiny into an embrace and slowly swept his fingers through her hair.

"Babe, you have no idea of the things I want to do to you," he declared as he stared intensely into her eyes. Then he kissed her mouth passionately.

Destiny could feel herself melting into Rick as her mind slowly caught up with her body. He smelt so good, a strong masculine scent of musk and whisky. He kissed with the same characteristic assertiveness with which he did business, and she was surprised at how good it felt to have him dominate her in this way.

Destiny's mom followed her from the sitting room to her bedroom. "Just because you have a music contract doesn't mean you're better than every one else, princess! Why don't you try actually helping me out for once in your life, and then we can talk about you becoming a superstar!"

"Why are you like this? What is wrong with you?!" Destiny exclaimed in sheer frustration and anger.

"Ha, you'll see one day! You'll see – when you have to live with a daughter who is a good-for-nothing, spoilt brat! Don't come running to me when that happens; I'll have no sympathy for you whatsoever!"

"I hate you!" Destiny yelled. "I wish you would just die so that you could leave me alone!"

"Well, why don't you just leave, huh?" her mother taunted. "I'm not stopping you! You are more than welcome to go!"

"You know what, Mom? I will! I never want to have to listen to you again!" Destiny screamed.

She grabbed a bag out of her closet and started throwing some clothes into it.

"So, where are you going to go princess?" her mom screamed with searing contempt.

"I don't care! All I care about is never having to hear the sound of your voice ever again!"

"Well, fine then, leave; see if I care! But I tell you what, when the police call me asking me to come fetch you, I won't come! You can rot in jail for all I care!"

Destiny grabbed the bag and stormed past her mom towards the door. Her mother followed her into the corridor and grabbed her by the arm.

"If you leave you aren't ever allowed to come back here!" she screamed.

"Good, because I never want to see your face again!" Destiny yelled, and wrenched her arm out of her mother's clasp. She walked out the door, slamming it behind her.

Destiny pressed Rick's doorbell. She knew that he had money, but still, this house was far nicer than she had even expected. She glanced around nervously, suddenly feeling very self-conscious. He answered the door swiftly.

"Destiny! This is a pleasant surprise," he said, looking a little confused. "What are you doing here?"

"My Mom," she exclaimed with a sob, "I just can't stand another day with that woman! Can I come stay with you, just for a while?"

"Yeah, sure," he responded, trying to process what she'd just said. "Come on in," he said, opening the door for her.

She walked into his living room, and observed that he was in the thick of work. His laptop was fired up and papers were strewn across the ottoman. As she glanced around she saw that the design of his home looked just like him: slick, modern, polished, impeccable.

"The bathroom's through there if you want to go wash your face, and you can drop your bag anywhere. I'll go make us some coffee."

Destiny turned to look at him, and as she did, she burst into tears. He rushed over to her and took her in his arms.

"Babe, don't cry, it's going to be ok!" he reassured her.

"She's just so evil! I hate her! I hate her so much!"

"Ssssh," he whispered in her ear, and then kissed her forehead. "It's going to be alright. You're safe here. You're safe with me."

She looked at him through tear stained eyes. "Do you love me?" she asked.

"Of course, babe, of course I love you," he reassured her.

She stared at him intensely, and then kissed him forcefully on the lips. To her surprise he responded equally passionately, kissing her with intensity and urgency that she had never yet seen him demonstrate before.

"Show me you love me," she commanded him, and challenged him with her eyes. He looked at her, and then kissed her hard, making it quite clear that he was the one in control.

He picked her up and carried her to his bedroom. He set her down on the bed and wildly kissed her neck. As he started to unzip the back of her dress he noticed that her body was shaking.

He looked her in the eyes. "Is this the first time?" he asked knowingly. She nodded slightly, and he ran his fingers through her hair. He kissed her gently.

As she started to relax he kissed her with a greater intensity of passion. She responded with equal measure.

Yeshua could feel the intensity of the sun burning through the clothing on his back. He staggered another step forwards, clouds of dust rising up in the hot dry air as he did so. For forty long days he had dwelled in this wilderness, in this lonely wasteland of rock and dirt. The voice had told him to come here, to dwell amongst the arid and barren landscape until his task had been fulfilled in that place. For forty days no food had passed his lips, as he sought to follow and hear the voice. Hunger consumed him and tormented him for his every waking moment. But he knew what the voice had told him, and so he continued to battle this temptation in his mind.

Relentless thoughts of relinquishing his task tortured him, and the temptation to simply go home was ever present.

The taunting thoughts were unending: "Who are you to think you can make a difference? What if you heard wrong? What if you imagined it all? What is being out here going to achieve? Why suffer — there's no point to this!"

Sometimes these thoughts were like a relentless fly, persistently buzzing around him. Then at other times they were like a vast army of attackers, with one legion after another tirelessly assaulting his mind. But he battled on, brutally striking down every one of these thoughts as they assailed him.

He took another step forwards and the ground started to spin. The sun was just so hot. Another step. If he could just eat. Another step. He tried to steady himself, but the dizziness hit him like a wall. He crumpled down on his knees as a wave of darkness enveloped him. His body fell across dirt, sending a cloud of dust up into the air as he hit the ground. The dust slowly settled, but he did not move.

"So this is the one they call the Savior!"

Yeshua slowly opened his eyes. His vision was blurry, but he already knew the identity of the one who was stood towering over him, peering down at him with contempt. It was The Tempter. The one he had been sent there to meet.

"Yet here you are, lying at my feet," The Tempter declared smugly as he walked around him in a circle, looking down at him with a mocking smile.

Yeshua placed his hands on the dirt and pushed himself up. Painfully, slowly, he stood and faced The Tempter.

The Tempter shook his head slowly. "I don't know...if you are truly the Savior, why do I find you lying here in your own filth, unable to even feed yourself? Surely, this is not how a Savior should live!"

"I will have my reward."

"But what if you are wrong? What if you are not the Savior? What if this has been a horrible mistake? Here," he picked up a stone and held it in front of Yeshua's face. "You look hungry. If you are truly the Savior, tell this stone to become bread."

Yeshua took the stone from him, and stared at it intensely. Then he looked up at The Tempter. "It is written, 'Man shall not live on bread alone'!" he responded, staring The Tempter in the eyes as he threw the stone away.

The Tempter narrowed his eyes. "Come with me, I have somewhere to show you," he declared. Yeshua conceded with a slight bow of his head.

At that very moment a whirlwind of light came upon them.

When it receded they stood on the edge of a tall building, the temple that Yeshua knew so well.

The Tempter pointed down at the ground below them, where people were congregating and going about their everyday business.

"If you are the Savior," he said, "throw yourself down here! For it is written 'He will command his angels concerning you to guard you carefully, they will lift you up in their hands, so that you will not strike your foot against a stone.' All these people would all see you being saved! They would all know that you are the Savior! Would this not be so much easier than what you're doing? You would never have to listen to anyone question you ever again!"

But Yeshua swiftly turned his back to the edge of the building and walked away from it. "It is also written: Do not put your Savior to the test!" he declared.

The Tempter sneered at him. "Come with me." Once more Yeshua bowed his head and the whirlwind of light came upon them. When it dissipated they were at the peak of a very high mountain. Below them lay all the kingdoms of the world, in all their beauty and splendor. Yeshua looked out over them and marveled at their magnificence.

The Tempter swept his hand across the horizon. "All this I will give you, if you will just bow down and worship me."

Yeshua looked at him, the fire of anger in his eyes. "Away from me, Tempter!" he ordered "For it is written: Worship the Savior, and serve him only!"

The Tempter snarled at him, and spoke in measured tones, "Clearly you have yet to see reason! We will meet again. And then, you will bow your knee to me."

And with that The Tempter departed, leaving Yeshua alone in the wilderness.

Yeshua collapsed once more on the ground. Hunger and exhaustion overwhelmed him. He was spent.

As he lay there motionless, a faint light became strong as many figures of light suddenly appeared around him.

They held him up and started ministering food and drink to his body, as the sound of many voices singing rang out across the barren landscape.

When Yeshua had finally regained his strength, he left the wilderness.

Chapter Four

I WALK THE LINE

"Are you sure it's a good idea?" Destiny asked the hairdresser, as she peered anxiously into the mirror.

"Honey, I've been doing this for twenty-three years and I can tell you that mousy brown has got to go. Are you serious about being a country star?"

"Yes."

"Well, then if you want to be a country star, you need to look like a country star."

"Okay," Destiny said, trying to sound more confident than she felt. She bit her bottom lip nervously. "It's just that if you could maybe make it not quite so black, I think I might feel a bit more comfortable with it."

"Listen, sweetheart, you're going to have to trust that I know what I'm doing, okay? Believe me, you're going to love the results."

"Okay. Of course. I'm sorry."

"No worries, honey. You just read that magazine and I'll have you looking beautiful in no time!"

She smiled nervously.

As Destiny looked over at the rack of clothes the stylist had picked out for her she realized that her hair was the least of changes she was going to be seeing that day.

"We should start with this, this and…oh…this," the stylist said as she rifled through the options at hand.

Destiny nodded silently and quickly took the chosen garments from the stylist. As she changed into them she could feel the stylists contented gaze.

"Oh, that looks amazing! Wow – look at that body! This outfit makes you look like a million bucks!"

She grabbed Destiny by the hand and dragged her in front of a full-length mirror.

"See how the high cut of the jeans accentuates that wonderfully slim waist of yours. And the V neck really brings the eyes down your body, which makes you look so much taller." The stylist looked at Destiny for a reaction. "What do you think – do you like it?"

Destiny just stared at her reflection in shock. She barely recognized the woman in the mirror.

"Yes. Yes, I think I do."

"Destiny, there's something I need to discuss with you," Bob Bailey said as he peered at her from behind his big, mahogany desk. As Destiny stared up at the rows of framed, gold records behind him, she realized that she would have very little say in whatever he was about to share.

"Your name has to go. Destiny Morgan, it's too mundane. We need a name that is high caliber, a name that you could see printed on t-shirts and in shining lights."

Destiny was stunned. The thought of changing her name had never even crossed her mind.

"Well, what do you want to call me?"

"Destiny Black."

"Destiny Black?"

"Yes, Destiny Black. It has a strength to it, a quality that fits you perfectly. Believe me, our marketing guys have put significant thought into this and we are absolutely confident that Destiny Black will be a successful name for you." He leaned back in his chair.

"Well, I guess you know best," she said in a slightly defeated tone.

Bob Bailey slapped the top of his desk in glee. "Yes we do, Destiny, yes we do!"

She smiled weakly.

He suddenly became sober and looked at her with a serious expression. "Destiny Morgan doesn't exist any more. From this day on, you're Destiny Black."

∽◯◯◯∽

Destiny walked into the dressing room, horribly nervous at the thought of the showcase that was shortly going to be starting. People from across the industry had been invited, and though much work had been put into preparing for this day she still had this terrifying thought in the back of her mind that she was going be discovered for being a fraud, and that it had all been some dreadful mistake.

She was expecting to have the dressing room to herself, and so was surprised to see a guy sat there chatting with the hair and make-up artist, who was touching up his hair as they conversed.

"I'm sorry, my name's Destiny Black, am I in the wrong room?" she asked.

The guy glanced over at her. "Oh no girl, you're cool. Me and Melinda, we go way back, we just catchin' up, that's all."

"Oh, okay. It's just that I'm already running a little late and I really think I should probably get ready."

"You're fine – you have plenty of time! You just sit down over there."

"Okay," Destiny said in an unsure voice, quietly sitting down as they picked up their gossip where they left off. She stared up nervously at the clock, whose handle was moving faster than she'd like.

She sat there for ten minutes, growing increasingly tense as they continued unabated, seemingly oblivious to her presence or her need. Eventually she plucked up the courage to speak again.

"I don't mean to be rude but I really need to get started," she interjected. Both the make-up artist and the man glanced over at her dismissively.

"Relax, princess, you have plenty of time," the man said disparagingly. He turned back to face the make-up artist.

"Well, I'm not sure I do," Destiny said, her nervousness making her voice tremble slightly.

"Well, that's too bad," the man said with a slight snort. The make-up artist glanced over at her with a slightly mocking air.

"You leave her alone, Jeremiah Andrews! And get your lazy butt out of that chair," a strong female voice ordered.

Destiny looked over, and she saw that a beautiful and defiant woman had just walked into the room. She looked older than Destiny – she was thirty maybe – and from her flaming red hair and bold attire Destiny had no doubt that she was a performer herself.

"No amount of time in that chair is going to do you the slightest bit of good Jeremiah, so you might as well get on out of it and apologize to this young woman before I come over there and make you do it."

"Yes, ma'am," he declared as he got up and unclipped the cloak the make-up artist had pinned on him. "Gee, I was just getting a little touch-up, there's no need to get so hostile!" he muttered as he stalked out of the room.

The woman walked up to the make-up artist and gave her a steely glare.

"Melinda, right?"

The make-up artist nodded.

"You know, you might want to think about how you deal with your clients. I'd really hate someone to tell this girl's management that she was made to wait while you sat around flirting with a roadie. Do you understand me?"

"Yes, ma'am," she replied. "It won't happen again."

"You're darn right it won't!" the woman retorted and strode out of the room, smiling triumphantly at Destiny as she did so.

❦

Though it was a little too early to know for sure, Destiny felt like her performance was well received. As she stood watching the audience from backstage, hope started to fill her that this was going to be the start of something big. She could feel the excitement rising.

"You know, if you're going to make it in this industry you're going to have to learn to stand up for yourself."

Destiny turned round and saw that the woman who had saved her in the dressing room was staring right at her.

"Gina Jackson," the woman said, as she held out her hand.

"Destiny Mor...Black," she replied, as she shook her hand.

"I'd heard great things about you, and tonight I found that they weren't telling lies. Dang girl, you've got a voice and a half!"

"Thank you," Destiny replied timidly. "If only I could get over these nerves!" she exclaimed.

"Oh, you don't worry about that. I'll teach you everything you need to know. I've been on the road singing country for half my life. Back-up, solo, studio, live; you name it, I've done it. What you have can't be taught, the rest…pfff…you'll soon pick it up."

"It's just such a different world than the one I'm used to," Destiny said self-consciously.

"Well girl, consider me your tour guide."

Yeshua sat at the wedding reception enjoying the fine food and the pleasant company. His mother was there, along with several of his close friends, and a good time was being had by all. A friend told a joke and he laughed heartily. He was just opening his mouth to respond with a quip when his mother suddenly interrupted him.

"Yeshua, can I speak with you briefly?"

He smiled at his friends. "I'll be back in a moment," he told them. Then he stood up and followed his mother out of earshot.

"Yeshua, they've run out of wine."

"I'm sorry to hear that."

"No, Yeshua, you don't understand, I'm asking you to do something about it."

"What would you like me to do about it?"

"I know you have the power to command anything to be. You have only to say the word and it will be done."

Yeshua looked at his mother with disbelief. "Mother, why do you involve me?" he exclaimed. "My hour has not yet come."

She searched his face knowingly and then simply shrugged her shoulders with a slight smile on her face. "Okay, son. Okay." She squeezed his arm and shot him another quick smile.

As she walked away she passed a couple of servants. "Do whatever he tells you," she commanded them, pointing discretely at him.

Yeshua sat back down at his table, ready to dive back into the conversation. But then out of the corner of his eye he caught a glimpse of the bride. She was so beautiful. Her delicate veil framed her radiant face as a frame would a masterpiece, and jewels adorned her wrists and neck. When she laughed her smile was as captivating as any sunset. Her beauty took his breath away. In that moment his heart was suddenly moved.

He looked around to see what was on hand, and he saw six large, stone water jars that looked like they could hold twenty to thirty gallons each. Closing his eyes, he waited for the voice to speak to him. And when it came to him, he knew what he needed to do. He immediately stood up and approached the two servants.

"Fill those jars with water," he ordered them, pointing at the jars.

The servants immediately got to work. They toiled diligently, quickly filling the jars to the brim.

"Now draw some out and take it to the master of the banquet," he instructed.

The servants looked hesitantly at the master of the banquet, unsure of what he would think of them presenting him with water. But when they looked back at Yeshua they knew that debate was not an option. So one of them quickly dipped a cup into the closest jar and carried it over to the master of the banquet.

Yeshua observed the proceedings from afar. He watched the master of the banquet bring the cup to his lips and drink deeply of it. He watched him suddenly call for the servant, who promptly brought the bridegroom to him. The master of ceremony was so emphatic that Yeshua could hear him declare from afar, "Everyone brings out the choice wine first and then the cheaper wine after the guests have had too much to drink, but you have saved the best till now!"

Yeshua smiled with amusement as the bridegroom accepted the compliment with a slightly confused look upon his face.

He turned to rejoin his table, and as he did so he suddenly realized that his friends were all staring at him with a stunned look upon their faces.

At that moment he knew there would be no going back.

Chapter Five

INSIDE YOUR HEAVEN

A feeling of pure euphoria swept through her entire body. Suddenly she felt so powerful, like she could do anything. All the anxiety she'd been feeling moments earlier had dissipated, and the residual sadness that was with her all the time was gone. Sheer bliss coursed through her veins. A warm, tingly sensation came into her limbs. Suddenly, everything was alright in the world.

"I told you you'd like it," Gina said with a smile. "Do some more," she suggested, handing Destiny the empty tampon applicator. Destiny took it and leaned carefully over the small mirror that lay on Gina's coffee table. She carefully inhaled a little more of the white powder, and then sat back.

It was sheer pleasure. Every part of her body felt happy. Her mind felt so calm. She closed her eyes, and felt like she was flying, soaring like an eagle.

"This is good stuff. Eddie only gets me the best," Gina said as she stretched her arms out in pleasure.

Destiny just gave her a dopey smile and closed her eyes again. This was what she'd wanted. This was what she'd been looking for. This was what she needed. This feeling of love. This feeling of peace. This feeling of being in harmony with the world.

Destiny had this incredible sensation of being in control, and she loved it.

Gina reached over to her iPod dock and put a song on. It was one of Destiny's favorites, currently top of the country charts. It sounded amazing. She'd never heard such amazing music in all her life.

In the next few days Destiny found that when she used, not only could she sing country, but she could write country. She wouldn't normally have had the courage to even pick up a pen to write, but this feeling of confidence and peace that the drug gave her made her feel invincible. And so she wrote. She wrote about her life, she wrote about her losses, she wrote about her passions, she wrote about her dreams. And when she presented her songs to Rick, he was genuinely surprised by their quality.

She recorded a couple of the songs on his phone for him to play for Bob Bailey, and shortly thereafter talks started in earnest of her using some of her own songs.

So she would spend hours sat on the floor of the sitting room, strumming her Dad's Guild Starfire, playing around with lyrics, finding hooks and beats. She was rapidly mastering the guitar, indeed it was as though all the lessons her father had given her so many years ago suddenly surfaced.

And thanks to the powder she had so much energy that she could just keep going for hours. She didn't get much sleep, but she really didn't seem to need it anymore. It didn't matter; it was a small price to pay, because she had what she wanted. She'd found an all-powerful, all encompassing, unconditional love, and she never wanted to go back.

Yeshua was on his way to the Galil with his friends. The religious leaders had heard of the incredible things he was doing, and their ardent disapproval meant it was no longer safe for him to remain in Y'hudah. They were rapidly passing through Shomron when they decided to stop at a small town called Sh'khem for supplies.

When they arrived on the outskirts of town Yeshua's friends headed into the city to buy food. As he was absolutely exhausted from the journey he chose to simply stay behind and rest.

Yeshua sat down in the shadow of a well to get some shelter from the harsh, midday sun. He quickly made himself comfortable as best he could, resting his back against the warm stone wall of the well. Then he closed his eyes and almost immediately drifted off into a light sleep.

After a while he was woken by the sound of soft footsteps approaching him. He slowly opened his eyes and saw that a young woman had come to draw water. She did not make eye contact with him, but simply went about her business with discretion.

The woman had a gentle but sensual beauty about her, with dark but flawless skin and startling blue eyes. She carried herself with confidence, and exuded an air of intelligence and youth.

Suddenly, out of nowhere Yeshua heard the voice break the silence. It sounded like thunder, and it startled him greatly.

It started to tell him about the woman that was before him. As he watched the woman go about her work he learned of her diligence, and of the heart of desire with which she had been pursuing him her whole life. He heard of how she hungered for even just a glimpse of truth, and of the many cruel difficulties she had faced in her life.

His heart filled with a burning love and compassion for her, and it overwhelmed him. He suddenly felt that he could not endure a single second more without speaking to her.

"Please, give me a drink," Yeshua asked her abruptly, interrupting her work.

The woman turned to look at him with surprise. He could see that she was taken aback, but he was not offended, for he knew that the men of Shomron rarely addressed women in public, indeed often not even their own wives. And he knew that it was most likely all the more surprising coming from a man of his heritage, as his people had few dealings with the people of Shomron.

"How is it that you, a Jew, ask for a drink from me, a woman of Shomron?" the woman asked, with a certain amount of fear in her voice.

Yeshua's lips curled in amusement. "If you knew the gift of God, and who it is that is saying to you, 'give me a drink', you would have asked him, and he would have given you living water!"

She looked confused. "Sir, you have nothing to draw water with, and the well is deep. Where do you get that living water? Are you greater than our father, Ya'akov? He gave us the well and drank from it himself, as did his sons and his livestock."

Yeshua could feel her earnest desire for truth in her words, and it pleased his heart. So he smiled, and pointed at the well. "Everyone who drinks of this water will be thirsty again, but whoever drinks of the water that I will give him will never be thirsty again. The water that I will give him will become in him a spring of water welling up to eternal life!"

The woman looked stunned. For the first time she looked at him right in the face. As she searched his eyes, he saw her expression suddenly change to one of transfixed hunger. He knew in that moment that she had seen the measure of love and compassion that he had for her.

"Sir, give me this water so that I will not be thirsty or have to come here to draw water!" she begged him.

Yeshua gave her a knowing look. "Go, call your husband, and come here."

The woman's gaze dropped. "I have no husband," she replied with a hint of shame.

Yeshua spoke softly, "You are right in saying, 'I have no husband', for you have had five husbands, and the one you now have is not your husband. What you have said is true."

The woman's head jerked up instantly as her eyes widened. "Sir, I perceive that you are a prophet!" she exclaimed. She then continued hesitantly, "Our fathers worshiped on this mountain, but you say that in Yerushalayim is the place where people ought to worship?"

"Woman, believe me, the hour is coming when neither on this mountain nor in Yerushalayim will you worship the Father. You worship what you do not know; we worship what we know, for salvation is from my people. But the hour is coming, and is now here, when the true worshipers will worship the Father in spirit and truth, for the Father is seeking such people to worship him. God is spirit, and those who worship him must worship in spirit and truth."

"I know that the Savior is coming!" the woman said with great conviction. "And when he comes, he will tell us all things!"

Yeshua responded with a broad smile filled with warmth and love. He looked at her intensely.

"I who speak to you am he!" he declared boldly.

The woman appeared shocked. For a moment he thought that she might turn from him. But she continued to stare into his eyes, and as she did so recognition started to wash over her face. Then joy filled her expression. And as the joy overwhelmed her she started to weep with happiness.

At that very moment Yeshua's friends returned with the food supplies. Their convivial banter came to a rapid end when they saw that he was speaking to a woman. He could tell from their faces that they were shocked to find him conversing with a woman, and a woman from Shomron no less. But they did not say a word.

The woman was so overwhelmed that she simply left her water jar and rushed back to the town to share what she had learned.

That night Yeshua could not sleep. It had been a busy day as the woman had brought many of her people to meet with him. Between the traveling and all the talking his body and his mind were exhausted. But sleep continued to elude him.

He got up and quietly slipped outside. The crowd had dissipated, and it seemed that everyone in the town but him were in the very depths of slumber. He made his way to a garden, and gently sat on a rock that lay under a tall tree. The full moon highlighted the buildings with an ethereal glow, and tranquility filled his heart as he surveyed the peaceful scene.

He pondered about the woman he had met that day. He recalled her faith, her courage and her strength. His heart swelled with joy at the knowledge of his newfound friendship with her.

And then a curious thing suddenly happened. As he held her face in his mind, a picture began to rapidly unfold before him. All of a sudden he saw the face of another woman. Then another. Then another. Then another. Their faces were beautiful, captivating, they took his breath away. As face after face appeared in front of Yeshua he was overcome by a love and a passion that drove him to his knees. Faces of women from every tribe, every nationality and every ethnicity appeared in rapid succession in front of him. He saw their beauty. He saw their pain. He saw their need, and he saw the passion of their desires. It overwhelmed him.

He started to sob, gut wrenching cries of pain and desire. As he bent over on his knees his heart was wrecked with a longing to reach these women, to heal these women, to bring them into the fullness of all they were designed to be. Yearning filled his soul.

"Father let me reach these women! Allow me to reach these women!" he cried into the cold, night air.

As he did so he felt his father's approval. And with that, he saw one last beautiful face.

He had met his Destiny.

Chapter Six

WHEN I GET WHERE I'M GOING

As she hit the top note she knew that it didn't sound pretty. Her throat hurt – it felt so raw that she couldn't help but wince as she strained her voice to hit that high. And from the look of the sound engineer, it hadn't gone unnoticed.

It had been six days since Destiny's voice had become hoarse – maybe seven – she couldn't remember. She coughed a shallow cough, hoping it wouldn't strain her throat too much, but even that caused a stab of pain.

"Let's try again," the sound engineer said over the intercom, without much enthusiasm.

She glanced at the door nervously. She couldn't wait to go lock herself in the bathroom and take a hit.

Destiny shook her body to the music. It didn't matter that there was no one at home to dance with her, she loved this song, she felt good and she was ready to party.

Suddenly her phone rang. She saw that it was Rick.

"Hey babe, when you coming home?" she asked him. "I was thinking, tonight we should go out dancing! I am so ready for some fun!"

"Destiny," he exclaimed in a menacing voice, "where are you?"

"I'm at home, Mr. Smarty Pants," she said, making fun of his serious voice.

"You were supposed to be in the studio forty-five minutes ago," he said in a low, threatening tone of voice. "The sound engineer is waiting for you, there are two executives that just so happened to have picked today to visit, and New Music Nashville are going to be here any moment!"

"Gee, sorry, there's no need to get so upset!" she retorted in a disparaging tone.

"Destiny, do you even realize how reckless you're being right now?!" he said, barely controlled frustration permeating his voice.

"Do you realize how uptight you're being right now?" she replied with annoyance. "Just chill out, ok. I just forgot; it's no big deal. I'll be there any minute."

"Destiny, I swear, you had better be sober when you get here," he exclaimed, anger percolating behind his every word.

"When did you get so boring?" she mocked.

"About the time you decided you were going to throw both our careers away by stuffing my bank account up your nose," he said in a near whisper.

"Fine, be like that," she said dismissively.

"Destiny, just don't leave the house, ok? I'm going to send a car to come pick you up."

"Okay, whatever," she said as she rolled her eyes, and hung up.

Destiny threw back another shot as Gina indicated to the bar man to bring them some more.

"They boss me around like I'm just such an idiot!" Destiny exclaimed. "This morning this one guy, this uptight suit who looks like he has a stick stuck up his butt, tells me that they're bringing in this writer to re-write my songs. So I'm all like, 'No, I don't want no one messing with my songs', but he tells me that I don't have a choice."

"You know sweetie, you have got to stop giving other people all the power. With a voice like yours you can do whatever you want. If they don't like you, don't worry, there'll be a dozen other places across town that will."

"That's easy to say," Destiny responded.

"No, seriously, you have to start playing the same game as them. If they intimidate you, then fine, intimidate them right back. Stop being pushed around by what everyone thinks! Besides which, who is this guy to tell you what you can or can't do? I mean, can he sing? No! Can he write? No! So he should just shut up and let you do what you do best."

"I guess you're right," Destiny said with a certain amount of resignation.

Gina swung round and grabbed her face in her hands.

"No — I am right!" she said forcefully. "You have to play as tough as everyone else, Destiny! Otherwise you're going to have people walking all over you, you hear me?"

"Okay, okay!" Destiny exclaimed, pulling herself out of Gina's grip. "I heard you – I'll play tough."

"As tough as everyone else," Gina stipulated.

"As tough as everyone else," Destiny repeated with mock dutifulness.

"There's a good girl!" Gina exclaimed, and knocked back another shot.

∾∾◦⌒◦∾∾

Destiny sat in the suit's office. As he went on and on the feeling of nausea that was in the pit of her stomach continued to increase. She looked around in desperation, hoping that he'd finish fast so that she could run to the bathroom and hurl.

But he wasn't finishing. He still had five more points that he wanted to go over. Destiny breathed in deeply, hoping to keep it together. Suddenly, she realized she couldn't hold off any longer. The content of her stomach abruptly rose into her mouth, and she lunged towards the wastebasket.

"What the…?!" the suit exclaimed in disgust.

Destiny wretched deeply. When she was done she wiped her face with her hand and glanced up sheepishly at the executive.

"Food poisoning," she said feebly.

"Yeah, right!" the suit said with disdain. "We'll see what Bob has to say about that!" He picked up his phone.

"What are you doing?!" Destiny shrieked.

"Calling your boss to tell him that you were so wasted that you couldn't even make it through a meeting without emptying your breakfast on my floor," he responded matter of factly.

"Stop!" Destiny ordered desperately.

"I don't take orders from junkies," the suit responded without batting an eye.

Destiny felt a rage rise in her as Gina's words suddenly came to her mind.

"If you don't stop I'm going to call your wife and tell her that you're sleeping with your assistant!" she threatened viciously.

The suit immediately froze and then turned to glare at her. From the look on his face Destiny could tell that her information was correct.

"You...what?!" the executive growled.

"You heard me. You make that call and I will tell your wife and children exactly what's going on when you take all those trips out of town. That is, unless you'd rather tell her yourself?" Destiny said in a nasty tone of voice.

"You wouldn't," the executive countered.

"Not if you don't!"

The suit stared at her appraisingly, and saw that she was for real.

"Fine then," he exclaimed through clenched teeth. "Nothing happened."

"Wonderful," she said with a smirk. "Then I guess I should be on my way. Unless there's more that you'd like to discuss?"

"No, I think this has been quite enough for one day," he said with barely controlled anger.

"Great!" she exclaimed, standing up. She walked over to the door, "Oh, and one more thing, I don't want anyone rewriting my songs. Are we clear?"

"Crystal clear," he said with seething contempt.

"Great! Well, have a nice day then."

Yeshua was teaching in a town in the Galil when he received a visit from two of Yochanan's close friends.

Yeshua was aware that Yochanan had been recently imprisoned by King Herod. Yochanan had condemned the King's decision to divorce his own wife in order to marry his brother's wife, Herodias. It was well known that Herodias nursed a grudge against Yochanan and wanted to kill him, but to date it seemed that Yochanan was at least protected by the King's curiosity in his strange sayings and righteous ways.

Yochanan's friends stood before Yeshua with a look of simultaneous defiance and weakness. Yeshua could tell that Yochanan's imprisonment had not been easy on them.

"Yochanan sent us to ask are you the one who is to come, or should we expect someone else?" one of the messengers declared, a slight hint of desperation creeping into his voice.

Yeshua was not surprised to hear this question. But it tugged at his heart none the less to know that Yochanan was doubting what he had witnessed at the river. He felt the cruel sting of betrayal, and he had to quickly rebuff the feeling of offense that rapidly assailed him. He knew that he needed to encourage his friend.

"Go back and report to Yochanan what you have heard and seen: The blind receive sight, the lame walk, those who have leprosy are cleansed, the deaf hear, the dead are raised and the good news is proclaimed to the poor. Blessed is anyone who does not stumble on account of me!"

The men exchanged glances, clearly aware of the weight of what was being said. They nodded swiftly, and then departed without another word, with the look of men that know their mission.

Yeshua simply looked into the distance. He thought of the freehearted Yochanan trapped in the darkness of a prison. He thought of the religious leaders that coveted his own death. And he thought of the many plots that were being mounted up against him.

The battle for Destiny had begun.

Some time later Yeshua was in Natzeret, the city where he had grown up. On Shabbat he went into the synagogue, as usual.

As Yeshua had been invited to speak, he stood before the congregation. The scroll of the prophet Yesha'yahu was handed to him. Unrolling it, he found the place where it is written:

"The Spirit of Adonai is on me, because he has anointed me to proclaim good news to the poor. He has sent me to proclaim freedom for the prisoners and recovery of sight for the blind, to set the oppressed free, to proclaim the year of the favor of Adonai."

After he had read this to the assembly he rolled up the scroll, handed it back to the attendant, and sat down. The eyes of everyone in the synagogue were glued to him.

"Today, as you heard it read, this passage of the Tanakh was fulfilled!" he boldly declared.

The audience gasped in shock. A ripple of murmurs ran through the crowd. "Where did this man get these things?" they whispered. "What's this wisdom that has been given him? What are these remarkable miracles he is performing? Isn't he just the carpenter? Isn't this Yosef's son?! Isn't this Miryam's son and the brother of Ya'akov, Yosi, Y'hudah and Shim'on?! Aren't his sisters here with us?! Where then did this man get all these things!"

Yeshua looked out across the assembled crowd. These were his people, the very community he had grown up with. And despite his many miracles, despite the heart of love he had shown them every day that he had dwelled with them, he saw that they still refused to recognize him as their Savior. He was both amazed and devastated at their lack of faith. Anger and sadness filled his heart and mind.

He addressed the crowd, "Surely you will quote this proverb to me: 'Physician, heal yourself!' And you will tell me to do here in my hometown what you have heard that I did in K'far-Nachum! Truly I tell you," he continued, looking round at the crowd, "no prophet is accepted in his hometown. I assure you that there were many widows in Isra'el in Eliyahu's time, when the sky was shut for three and a half years and there was a severe famine throughout the land! Yet Eliyahu was not sent to any of them, but to a widow in Tzarfat in the region of Tzidon! And there were many in Isra'el with leprosy in the time of Elisha the prophet, yet not one of them was cleansed — only Na'aman the Syrian!"

The synagogue erupted with a roar of furious rebukes.

"This is blasphemy! He is deluded! Who are you to insult us?! Who are you to look down upon us?!" they yelled with indignation as they waved their fists at him in anger.

Two men grabbed hold of Yeshua and dragged him out of the building, as the crowd followed behind. Dragging him through the streets, the crowd became increasingly impassioned and fervent in their anger.

They reached the brow of the cliff on which the town was built, and were ready to throw him off the edge. But in the commotion they became very confused and Yeshua was able to quickly slip out of his captors' grasp.

He walked right through the crowd, and went on his way.

As Yeshua walked away from the town his heart was heavy. He knew that if these people, the very people who had known him his whole life, were willing to utterly reject him, there was no guarantee that Destiny would accept him either. But he knew that he had to do whatever it took to reach her, even if after paying the ultimate price she still did not receive his love.

He resolved to fight even harder for her heart.

One morning Yeshua sat outside praying quietly when he saw two of Yochanan's closest friends appear in the distance. As soon as he saw the looks on their faces, he already knew what news they were bringing.

"Yeshua, we came with news of Yochanan," one of them declared. There was an awkward pause. "We regret to tell you that he is no longer of this earth. He was beheaded at King Herod's orders."

Even though he had known what they were going to say, Yeshua felt the shock hit him like a wave.

"When?" he asked.

"Two days ago. We gather that Herod's daughter asked for his head on a plate, a favor manipulated by Herodias herself, no doubt. It seems Herod had declared publicly that his daughter could ask for anything that she wanted and that he would give it to her. So when she asked for Yochanan's head he could not say no."

Yeshua simply sat there for a moment, quietly absorbing this information. Then he looked up at the men.

"Thank you for coming to share this with me," he said, with great sincerity.

Both men simply bowed their heads solemnly and departed without another word.

Yeshua looked up at the sky that was so perfectly blue. He knew that a day was coming soon when a great darkness would fall upon him too.

"Father," he declared, "give me the strength to see your purposes through." He searched the sky, and then sighed deeply.

He knew that saving Destiny was going to cost him his all.

Chapter Seven

PICTURE TO BURN

Destiny looked out across the audience as she strummed her guitar. The audience was larger than she had anticipated, certainly larger than for her last few performances. She scanned the faces, searching for the only one she really cared about in that moment.

There he was, in the back row.

He didn't look a day older than the last time she'd seen him. He was encouraging her with his smile and miming to her to remind her of where to place her hands for the chords.

She closed her eyes for a moment. When she opened them, he was gone.

It didn't matter. He'd be at her next performance.

Destiny sat in Bob Bailey's office with Rick. The atmosphere was somber.

"The bottom line is, they've changed their minds. They don't want her on the tour and there's no talking them out of it," Bob declared.

"What about the Summertime Rush tour?" Rick asked.

"I already put the call in. They're not interested."

"Well can't we make them interested?"

"Sure, we could, if your big superstar could actually manage to be on time every once in a while and not mess up her lyrics on stage."

"That was a one time thing!" Destiny interjected.

"Damn well better be!" Bob exclaimed.

"Okay, okay, I'll put some calls in with Kyle this afternoon," Rick said. "I've got some good pull with him, and I know he hasn't made any decisions about his tour yet, so it's worth a shot."

"Make me happy, Rick," Bob ordered.

"Will do, Sir," Rick declared assertively.

Rick stood up, and Destiny followed. They left the office, and headed out towards the parking lot. As they got into Rick's car, Destiny could feel his anger raging.

"It's not that bad," she exclaimed. "I'm probably going to end up getting a much better deal anyway."

"Are you kidding me?!" Rick roared as he slammed his hand on the car wheel. "Are you absolutely out of your mind?!"

"Okay, sorry!" she said, bemused. "I just don't think it's that big of a deal, is all. You'll figure it out, you always do."

"Woman, you're killing me!" he exclaimed. "Do you have any idea how hard it is to put a deal like that together?! Weeks of work down the drain, for nothing! And all because you're a filthy cokehead!"

"Well, maybe I wouldn't need it so bad if you weren't chasing skirt all the time!" she shrieked, quickly spiraling out of control. "You think I don't know what you're up to, huh?! You don't think I hear the stories?! I know you're cheating on me!"

"You're out of your frigging mind!" he yelled. "The coke has made you mad!"

"Well I don't have to be crazy to know that a cheater is always a cheater! And I know what you are, Rick!"

"I swear, you speak one more word and you're going to regret it," he threatened in a low and menacing voice.

"I'm not afraid of you," she said with contempt.

He sat there clenching his jaw as she just stared resolutely ahead. After a few moments, his face softened. He breathed out deeply.

"Listen babe, I'm sorry, okay. I just got mad because I'm frustrated about the tour, okay? You know I'm not cheating on you! Lets just go home, chill out and forget about all this."

She turned to look at him.

"Just you and me?" she asked.

"Yes, babe, we can do anything you want to do."

"Okay, let's go home."

***

Destiny ripped open the magazine. There it was – a full two page profile on her. The photograph looked great, an intense shot of her holding her father's guitar over her head, staring straight into the lens of the camera. She avidly devoured the article.

But when she got to the last paragraph she suddenly felt like someone had thrown a bucket of ice water over her. There, in stark black and white, was a nasty, snarky journalistic barb about her looks.

She suddenly felt self-conscious, naked, exposed. A horrible feeling gripped her from the inside out.

She softly padded into the living room, where Rick was engrossed in responding to an email.

"Babe," she said questioningly.

"Yeah," he said in a distracted tone of voice.

"Do you think I'm pretty?"

"Eh…what?" he asked, looking up.

"Do you think I'm pretty?" she asked, in a tone that was both demanding and needy.

"Yeah, you're pretty," he said in a flat tone. He returned to typing his email. "But not beautiful," he continued.

Destiny felt like she'd just been shot in the heart. For once, she didn't have a word to say.

***

"Sweetie, don't sweat it, you're gorgeous," Gina reassured her as she picked a pair of jeans off of the store rail. "Think about it this way, these people, they're just jealous! They don't have half the raw talent you do, and so they're just trying to grind you down. And it's not going to be the last time that happens to you in this industry! So you just got to learn to say screw them and move onto the next thing."

"I just feel so bad. This morning I was going to have a bagel for breakfast, and then all I could think about is that I'm ugly and fat and that if I eat the bagel I'm going to get even fatter!" Destiny responded.

"Oh hon, just relax okay? You want to eat a bagel? Eat a bagel! If you're worried about getting fat there are ways to deal with that."

"Like what?" Destiny asked.

"You know…" Gina hinted expressively with her eyes.

"No…" Destiny said, confused.

Gina mimed sticking her hand in her mouth and making herself vomit.

"Just get rid of it when you're done. It's easy."

Destiny gasped with shock. "Eeew…that's gross! Who would do that?!"

"Sweetie, there's no need to act so high and mighty. How do you think I stay looking this good?"

"Seriously?! You do that to yourself?!" Destiny asked in disbelief.

"Like, every other day. Listen, it's really no big deal. Everyone does it. It's like flossing your teeth. What's the worst that's going to happen?"

"Well, nothing, I guess," Destiny responded timidly.

"Okay, well just enjoy yourself then. You only live once, so stop being so hard on yourself! And you have got to try these on," she said, passing Destiny a pair of skinny cut jeans. "You are going to look to–die–for in them!"

❧❧❧❧❧❧❧

Yeshua was in the region of Tzor and Tzidon with friends when a woman from Kena'an approached him pleading, "Lord, Son of David, have mercy on me! My daughter is demon-possessed and suffering terribly!"

Yeshua did not answer a word.

His friends urged him irately, "Send her away, she keeps yelling at us!"

Yeshua looked at her compassionately. "I was sent only to the lost sheep of Isra'el," he explained to her gently.

She threw herself before him, kneeling in the dirt. "Sir, help me!" she begged.

"It is not right to take the children's bread and toss it to their pet dogs," he responded with concern.

"That is true, sir," she said. "But even the dogs eat the crumbs that fall from their master's table!"

Yeshua was taken aback. He knelt down to look her in the face. In her eyes he saw such faith and strength. She reminded him of the woman that Destiny was made to be, and it moved his heart.

"Lady, you are a woman of great trust!" he exclaimed. "Let your desire be granted."

"Thank you! Thank you!" she exclaimed, as she turned away to rush home with expectancy.

As he watched her depart Yeshua anticipated the day when he would finally end Destiny's torment too.

Chapter Eight

YOUR CHEATIN' HEART

Destiny flushed the toilet and went to the sink to rinse her mouth out. She looked at herself in the mirror. Her usually pearly white teeth looked a little yellow.

She reassured herself that no one would notice.

Her throat felt horrendously dry. She swallowed another mouthful of water in the hope that it would remedy it, but it did little good, so she left the bathroom in search of some ice.

As she crossed the living room the room suddenly started spinning. She stumbled and caught hold of the side of the sofa, and dropped down onto her knees. It felt like the floor was coming up at her. She tipped over onto her side and collapsed onto the floor, digging into the rug with her fingers.

"I've got a long list of real good reasons for all the things I've done…I've got a picture in the back of my mind of what I've lost and what I've won…I've survived every situation…knowing when to freeze and when to run…and regret is just a memory written on my brow…and there's nothing I can do about it now…" circled round and round in her mind as the room spun.

Rick walked through the front door some time after 8pm. Destiny sat watching TV, mindlessly flipping through the channels as she sipped a large glass of wine.

"Busy day?" he asked with a hint of contempt.

"Yeah," she answered in a distracted tone of voice, momentarily engrossed in something the news anchor was saying.

Rick took off his jacket and pulled off his shirt. "Babe, I'm just going to jump in the shower okay?" he said as he headed to the bathroom.

"Yeah, sure," she responded, without really listening.

She could hear the sound of the shower being turned on full force. She changed the channel again.

Suddenly Rick's phone started vibrating in his jacket pocket. A text message. She ignored it. Then it vibrated again.

Her mind started to think about all the people it could be. She started to think about the many women she knew wanted to have their way with Rick, all the women she knew he flirted with behind her back. Dark thoughts started creeping into her mind and her heart started beating with pure adrenalin.

She put down the remote and carefully listened to the noise coming from the bathroom. Then she carefully slipped her hand into the jacket pocket, and slid his phone out.

Her heart pounding, she read the first message.

"BTW, next time call me first."

It was from a number she didn't recognize.

She quickly moved onto the second message. Same number.

"Rick baby you rock my world. Had the best time last night."

Destiny grabbed the phone in her fist and slammed down her glass of wine on the coffee table. She stormed over to the bathroom and threw open the door. Rick stood in the shower with his back turned to her. When she spoke she could barely control her rage.

"Babe, how did that meeting with Kevin go last night?" she asked.

"Good, I think he liked what I had to say. He's a clever guy, you know, smart."

"So it was just the two of you then?"

Rick picked up the shampoo and poured some in his hand, barely paying her attention. "Uh huh," he said, as he rubbed some of the shampoo into his hair.

"And what did you do after that?" Destiny asked.

"I came home." He suddenly paused and turned to look at her. "Why you asking?" he asked suspiciously. "I told you I was meeting with Kevin."

"Oh, I don't know," she said, as she casually walked up to the shower. She suddenly wrenched the door open. "Maybe it's because some slut just texted you some skanky messages about how you were with her last night!"

She threw the phone right at Rick with all her might.

"Ouch!" he exclaimed. "What the hell?! What is wrong with you, woman?!"

"Who is she?!" Destiny shrieked. "Tell me who she is!"

"It's probably a wrong number you crazy bitch!" Rick yelled.

"Then why did she use your name, huh?! You think I'm some kind of idiot?! What's her name?! Where did you meet her?!"

"Just shut up, Destiny! Leave me alone!" Rick hollered.

"I'll leave you alone when you tell me her name! What's her name?! What's her name?!" Destiny screamed, completely out of control.

"Shut up!"

"What's her name?!"

"Shut up! Just shut up!"

"What's her name?!"

Suddenly Rick snapped, and smacked Destiny in the face with all his strength. She flew backwards, catching the back of her head on the wall behind her. She slumped over from the shock, just managing to steady herself from the impact before she hit the floor. Her head reeled from the blow.

Rick stared at her, horrified. For a split second they both just froze, immobilized in shock.

"Oh my God!" he exclaimed. "Destiny, I didn't mean to do that! I'm sorry! I'm so sorry, baby!"

Destiny glared at him as pain seared through her head. She started shaking her head, her thinking shot to pieces from the physical pain that was now ripping through her skull, and the anger that was raging in her mind.

She turned to walk away from him, but he grabbed her arm.

"Destiny, I didn't mean to do that!" he exclaimed.

"Damn right you didn't!" she retorted, as she pulled herself free from his grip. She stormed out into the corridor as he jumped out of the shower and followed her, shampoo still on his head.

"Destiny, don't go!" he begged. "I can explain!"

She just grabbed the car keys, shot him a nasty look, and walked out the door, slamming it shut behind her as she did so.

As she downed her Jack Daniels, it occurred to her that really, over the years, Jack had probably been her most loyal friend. She grinned drunkenly at the irony, and crunched on an ice cube with her teeth. She loved crunching ice cubes.

The guy sat next to her glanced over at her.

"So what's a girl like you doing in a place like this?" he asked with a cheeky grin. She burst into drunken laughter. This guy was funny.

"Just trying to forget what a jackass my boyfriend is," she responded with a glib smile.

"Well, he must be a real jackass if he's leaving you to be preyed on by the likes of me," the guy said with a grin as he took a swig of his beer.

"I don't think he's too worried about that right now," Destiny said with a slight sneer. "He's probably got his hands all over some girl as we speak."

"Well, that's a pretty shame for him. Why do you let him treat you that way?"

"I dunno, I was just trying to figure that out myself."

"Maybe he ain't that bad."

"Ha," she rolled her eyes expressively and then looked over at him. "Just today he swears to me blind that he was in a business meeting last night, but guess what, there's some text message from some slut about how great of a time they had last night. He's that bad, alright."

The guy took another swig of his beer. "Well, as far as I see it you got two choices. You can either sit here feeling real bad for yourself, right? You can nurse your wounds with alcohol, get a little angry, feel miserable. But that ain't really going to hurt him much, is it?" He paused for dramatic effect. "Or," he continued "you could get your own back on him."

"What do you mean?"

"You know, play the same game, by the same rules. I mean, if he's going to have some fun, you might as well too."

Destiny suddenly realized what he was hinting at. "That's not really my style," she informed him curtly.

"Maybe it's not. But maybe it should be. I mean, indulge me for just one moment. Just think about how good it would feel to do to him exactly what he's done to you. Don't you think it'd feel good to know that you'd given back just as good as you'd gotten? It's just my opinion, but I think that sure beats sitting in some smoke ridden bar feeling sorry for yourself."

"And I suppose that you propose to be my kind benefactor?" Destiny said in a slightly mocking tone.

He put down his beer and looked her square in the eyes. "I'd pay you," he said.

"What the…!" she suddenly exclaimed. "I'm no hooker!"

"Woah, woah, woah sweetheart," he chided. "No need to get all uptight! All I'm saying is that you want to get your own back on this jackass, right? So, you already know what you're going to do, what anyone here could already tell you you're going to do. So you may as well get paid for it, right? Listen, I'm a good man, it's not like I'm out on the streets looking for women. But you know, it's just common sense. I got a need, and you got a need. So what's the harm in everyone getting what they need?"

Destiny just sat there for a moment, trying to think clearly through the haze of liquor and the pain that was pumping from the back of her head. She knew she wasn't that kind of girl. But then again, the guy had a point. If she was going to do it, she might as well get paid, right?"

He shot her a look. "So what do you say hon, you ready to have some fun?" he challenged.

She drained her glass.

"Where are we going?" she asked.

"My car is parked round the back," he said with a grin.

按按按按

At daybreak Yeshua came to the temple. All the people gathered around him, and so he sat down to teach them.

Suddenly there was a great commotion and the sound of many footsteps as angry voices approached. Yeshua looked up and was greeted with the sight of some of the local religious leaders dragging a woman towards him. She was protesting and yelling desperately.

When they reached him they threw the woman at him. She stumbled and fell to the floor. She made no attempt to get back up, so one of them yanked her to her feet.

"Teacher, this woman has been caught in the act of adultery," one of the men declared. "In our Law, Moshe commanded that such a woman be stoned to death. So what do you say about it?"

Yeshua calmly scanned their faces. He could tell from their expressions of barely concealed glee that they were testing him. Anger welled up in him. But he knew that self-control was of the utmost importance before these men, and so he channeled his anger into the only force he knew they would respond to – intellect.

He didn't say a word, but instead silently stared at them with an appraising gaze. Then he bent down and wrote on the ground with his finger. The crowd burst into a cacophony of whispers as people speculated on what he was writing.

"What do you say, teacher?" the leader insisted, as some of his group tried to subtly read what was being written. When Yeshua failed to answer him he insisted once more "What do you say?!"

Yeshua looked up at the man, rose to his feet, and then stared at him right in the eyes.

"The one of you who is without sin, let him be the first one to throw a stone at her," he declared.

The leader was shocked. He glanced uneasily at his cohorts, but they simply stood there nervously awaiting instruction.

Yeshua shot each of them a knowing look, and once more bent down to write on the ground as the crowd looked on.

Suddenly one of the men who had dragged the woman in there, an older man, turned and walked rapidly away. Then a couple of the older cohorts joined him. A ripple of whispers broke through the crowd.

The younger men stood there for a while longer, unsure of what to do. But after a few moments the intensity of the crowd's gaze upon them was just too much, and so they too departed rapidly, leaving Yeshua alone with the woman.

Yeshua stood up and stared at the woman. Her hair had fallen in her face, and so she swept it back into place as she brushed the tears from her eyes. As she did so Yeshua saw the splendor of her face. The depth of her beauty stunned him to silence.

As he looked in her eyes he could see the reflections of women he had seen that night in the garden of Sh'khem. In her he saw their magnificence. In her he saw their pain. In her he saw Destiny.

It made him want to reach into the darkness of hell itself to wipe away her pain.

"Woman, where are they? Has no one condemned you?" he asked with a slight smile.

She looked in his eyes briefly, and then spoke in what was barely a whisper, "No one, Lord."

"Neither do I condemn you," Yeshua said gently. "Now go, and don't sin any more."

The woman nodded rapidly, suddenly overcome with emotion. With tears flowing down her face she fled, free to live once more.

As he watched her leave, the desire swelled in Yeshua's heart for the hour when he would rescue all the women he'd seen reflected in her eyes. He longed for the day when he would give each and every one of them a second chance. He longed for their liberation. He longed for their freedom. And he longed for the moment when he would finally tell Destiny just how much he loved her.

Chapter Nine

SHE WOULDN'T BE GONE

Destiny sat on the side of the bathtub, breathing in deeply. The line she'd just done had made her feel really weird. The feeling probably wasn't helped by the fact that she hadn't slept properly in days. She felt exhausted, drained and miserable, and the coke she'd just inhaled was barely making a dent in it.

She returned to the bedroom and crawled back into bed. Rick had left for work a while ago; she wasn't too sure when. She pulled the covers over her head. The darkness felt good. The nothingness felt good. She wished that she could just melt away into it.

She didn't feel like she had the energy to do anything. It just all felt too overwhelming, too much. All she wanted to do was lie there and just be.

She curled her hands into fists, unintentionally pressing her nails into her soft, tender skin. As she felt the pain, a flood of relief suddenly washed over her. So she did it again. This time she pressed her nails into the joints of her fingers. A feeling of calmness came upon her, of being in control. She felt safe. It felt good.

The sound of the phone ringing woke Destiny out of the deepest of sleeps. She sat up slowly, feeling utterly groggy and disoriented. She looked over at the clock – it was 5:40pm. She hadn't planned to fall asleep.

By the time she reached her phone it had stopped ringing. It was Bob Bailey. She realized with alarm that she'd missed four phone calls from him that day.

At that very moment Rick walked through the front door. He entered the room and looked at her with unbelief.

"Have you been here all day?!" he asked frostily, clearly already aware of what the answer was going to be.

"I just didn't realize it was so late, okay?" she said, self-consciously.

"Destiny, Bob has been trying to call you all afternoon!"

"Well, my phone is having problems alright!" she said defensively.

Rick shot her the coldest of looks. "Bob's dropping you Destiny. You're finished."

"What do you mean? I don't understand," she said, trying to think clearly through the haze that was enveloping her mind.

"You're done Destiny. You're through. You've successfully managed to alienate all our key contacts. Elite have had enough of you missing meetings. They've had enough of you being so wasted you can barely stand on stage. And they've had enough of your absolutely obnoxious behavior."

"But surely there's been a mistake?!" Destiny said. "I'm not that bad!"

"Destiny, do you even hear yourself?" Rick exclaimed. He ran his hands through his hair in sheer frustration. "I am so, so, so fed up of this, I swear I can't take it any more!"

Destiny crawled off the bed and walked over to him.

"No, baby, no! It's not that bad! You'll see, this will just blow over, it always does! Everything's going to be fine! Just tell me you love me," she begged.

He looked at her with such contempt it made her reel.

"I'm going out. And when I get back, I want you gone."

"No, baby, no!!!" she begged, but it was too late. He pulled away from her and started towards the door. She ran after him, clawing at him and trying to get him to respond.

"Stop! Stop!!! It's all going to be okay!" she cried. "I'm going to be famous, Rick! We're going to be famous, you and me!"

He shrugged her off abruptly. "I don't want to see you anymore, Destiny! Go get your stuff and get out of here!" he yelled.

But she continued to pull at him as he opened the door, and all the way to his car. He pushed her away harshly, and proceeded to get into his car. She collapsed on the ground, sobbing, as he quickly pulled out of the drive.

"No, baby, don't go! I need you! I need you!!!" she sobbed.

She sat there crying and hyperventilating. After a while she got cold, and so she dragged herself back inside. She stumbled to the bedroom and started searching frantically for her phone. She finally found it on the floor by the bed and quickly dialed it.

"Bob?"

"Destiny I've been trying to reach you all day! Where the hell have you been?"

"Rick told me, he told me that you don't want me any more! I know that I might have messed up some stuff, but I promise you I won't do that any more. I need a second chance Bob. Please give me a second chance!"

"I've already given you a second chance Destiny. And a third chance. And a fourth chance. And a fifth chance. I'm sorry, but I'm done."

"But I need this. I need this!" she cried.

"I'm sorry," he said firmly.

"Please, I'll do anything!" she begged.

"Destiny I'm at dinner with friends and there's really nothing more I can do about this. I'm sorry it didn't work out, but that's just the way it is."

"But I can come meet you where you are! We can talk some more!" she exclaimed.

"Destiny, just do yourself a favor, get yourself into rehab, okay? You need help."

Destiny suddenly got really mad.

"You know what, I don't need you! I don't need you, you hear me?! Screw you! Screw you, Bob!" she yelled, and hung up the phone. As soon as she'd done so she realized that she had made a mistake. She dialed his number again. It went to voicemail.

She started to panic, alternating between sobbing and hyperventilating. She quickly dialed another number.

"Gina?"

"Woah, what's wrong, girl? You sound rough!"

"Gina, Elite just cut me, and Rick is kicking me out, and I don't know what to do!" she wailed hysterically.

"Elite cut you?" Gina asked.

"Yeah, they just came out of nowhere with this! Just like that, they told me it's all over! I don't understand, it's like there's been a mistake!"

"I doubt it," Gina said rather bluntly.

"Well, can I stay with you? Just for a while, just till this all gets fixed," Destiny asked between sobs.

There was a silence on the line.

"Gina? Gina can you hear me?"

"Yes, I can," Gina said reluctantly.

"So is it okay if I come round tonight?"

"I don't think that's going to work, Destiny."

"What do you mean?! What do you mean, Gina? Where else am I supposed to go?!" Destiny hollered.

"Well, I guess you should have thought of that before you pissed everyone off," Gina said in an uncompassionate tone of voice.

"What?!" Destiny exclaimed.

"Honestly Destiny, if you can't keep it together I don't think I really want to hang out with you right now."

Destiny was shocked. It took her a moment to be able to speak.

"You know what, screw you too! I hope you go to hell!" she shrieked. She hung up and threw her phone on the bed.

Destiny felt like she was going to explode with anger and rage. She grabbed the bed frame and jilted the bed violently. Then she grabbed a book off of the bedside table and threw it against the wall, screaming almost incoherently as she did so. She grabbed a clock and threw it at the other side of the room. It broke into pieces, sending glass and plastic flying across the room. Then she picked up her father's guitar, which had been sitting in the corner of the room. Without a moments hesitation she smacked it repeatedly against the wall, smashing it to pieces as she did so.

She collapsed on the floor and burst into tears. Her whole body shook as she sobbed. She just cried and cried until she could cry no more.

After a while she felt completely emotionally drained. A dull sense of pain and resignation took hold of her, and she simply sat there staring at the wall, emotionally spent.

She looked at the floor, at the debris of glass and wood that littered the carpet. For a while she just stared at it.

Then she picked up a shard of glass. It was long and thin, and she guessed it was probably from the glass of wine she'd been drinking earlier. She ran her finger along its razor sharp edge. A feeling of calmness came over her.

Without a second thought, she pressed the sharp edge of the glass hard against her wrist.

Yeshua's friends showed him the donkey they had brought.

"Did you have any trouble?" he asked them.

"Not much," one of them replied. "There were some people standing there who asked us what we were doing when we were untying it. We just did exactly as you said and told them you needed it and that we'd send it back to them shortly, and they let us go."

"It was just where you told us it would be, outside on the street tied in that doorway!" one of them exclaimed.

One of the men then threw his cloak over the donkey.

Yeshua climbed onto the donkey. He felt his heart beating fast. He knew that some of the religious leaders had already given orders that anyone knowing his whereabouts should inform them, so that they could arrest him. And now he was about to ride into their midst. But he was ready. It was time to go win Destiny's heart forever.

A vast crowd was congregating outside the city walls. Yerushalayim was buzzing with activity from the masses that had descended on the city for the festival of Pesach, but when people heard that Yeshua was on his way the ranks swelled even more. Word of his arrival spread like wildfire, as many who had witnessed him do strange and marvelous things were spreading the word through the city streets and surrounding countryside fast. Many were speculating as to what this all meant.

People started bringing branches they had cut in the fields to lay on the ground in front of him, while others spread their cloaks on the road. They lined the streets in a frenzy of anticipatory excitement, and started shouting:

"Blessed is the coming Kingdom of our father David!"

"Blessed is he who comes in the name of Adonai!"

"Hosanna in the highest heaven!"

"Blessed is the King of Isra'el!"

As Yeshua appeared in the distance riding on the donkey the crowd roared with applause and well wishes. As he rode past them they tried to touch him, to touch the donkey, to get close to him by any means possible. The crowd enveloped him, making his progress forwards both slow and boisterous.

Some religious leaders on the edges of the crowd scowled at the scene. One of them pushed his way in towards Yeshua, and when he was sufficiently close yelled at him "Teacher, rebuke your followers!"

Yeshua looked down at him from the donkey. "I tell you," he replied, "if they keep quiet, the stones will shout!"

The leader was perplexed and frustrated at his reply. He turned his back to Yeshua and fought his way out of the crowd. When he reached his cohorts he shook his head with disapproval and said "See, this is getting us nowhere! The whole world is following him!"

"Who is this?" a peasant who stood close by asked, pointing at Yeshua.

A man in the crowd informed him breathlessly, "This is Yeshua, the prophet from Natzeret in the Galil!"

The religious leaders exchanged looks of deep displeasure.

As Yeshua violently knocked the table over coins and equipment flew across the ground. The noise of metal and wood clanging on stone resonated across the temple court. Men hurled insults at him while women screamed. He quickly moved to the next table, picked it up with his bare hands, and furiously threw it across the yard. It broke in two as splinters of wood flew in every direction. Onlookers fled in fear, astonished and terrified by the mad man in their midst.

A searing anger consumed Yeshua as he glared around the people assembled in the courtyard.

At that very moment an unsuspecting man walked in holding a crate of merchandise. Yeshua saw him, and roared with anger. The man looked up, and saw the rage that was being directed towards him, and the chaotic scene of tables and benches that had been destroyed and thrown in just about every direction. He quickly swung around and dashed down out of the courtyard, as merchandise toppled out of his crate and onto the floor.

Yeshua turned back to look at the people assembled, all of

which were in various states of shock.

"It is written," he cried, "My house will be called a house of prayer! But you are making it a den of robbers!"

The crowd stared at each other uncomfortably. Some of them just looked annoyed, while others looked scared. A few looked ashamed.

Yeshua looked at these people, these treacherous, evil people who had perverted a place of holiness for money and power. Oh, how he abhorred their cowardice! How he hated their usury!

He looked up at the sky and thought of Destiny. He thought of how she needed a home to come to, a place where she could be safe, and truly loved. This was his provision for her! But instead these people had turned this place into a nest of thieves and vipers.

From far away a group of religious leaders witnessed this scene. From that moment they began earnestly looking for a way to murder Yeshua.

Chapter Ten

THE HOUSE THAT BUILT ME

Destiny opened her eyes. She was in a room she didn't recognize. The light was harsh, and the mattress hard. She felt weak.

She turned her head slightly, and saw a woman sat by her bedside reading a magazine. The woman glanced up and saw that Destiny was awake. She put down her magazine.

"Where am I?" Destiny whispered.

"You're at St. Thomas hospital," the woman answered. "You tried to kill yourself."

Destiny tried to think back. Her memory was hazy. She remembered flashing lights…smashing a guitar against a wall…sirens. She looked down weakly, and saw that both wrists were tightly wrapped in thick bandages.

"Who found me?" she asked feebly.

"Your cleaner. She came in to pick up some keys, and found you lying there. You're extremely fortunate that she found you when she did. Someone up there must really care about you!"

Destiny just looked away and just stared at the wall. Surely if there was anyone up there they hated her.

"Is Rick here?" she asked anxiously.

"No. No honey, he's not."

Destiny felt a wave of despair hit her.

"I'm going to sit with you here for a while," the woman continued. "Tomorrow one of my colleagues is going to come meet with you to discuss some options for therapy that we think could be beneficial."

Destiny just grimaced a little. She continued to stare at the wall with resignation.

"I need to sleep," she said, and closed her eyes.

Destiny hated every day she spent at the hospital. The staff were kind to her, but she couldn't stand their so-called helpful suggestions. Their concern annoyed her; she knew she didn't need their help. So by the time her wrists had started healing and she'd regained her strength she was more than ready to leave.

When she was discharged she was half hoping that Rick would be there to greet her. Every day of her stay at St. Thomas she had asked the nurses if he had rung, or if they'd seen him, only to be met with the same expression of concern and the news that no, they had not heard from him.

As her clothes had been destroyed when she'd reached the hospital, they'd kindly supplied her with an outfit to go home in. Home…where was that now?

Miraculously the cleaner had somehow seen fit to give Destiny's handbag to one of the ambulance men, so she at least had her purse and her credit card. She called a taxi from the nurse's station. When they arrived she asked them to take her to a motel she'd often seen driving down the I-40.

When she arrived at the motel she could see why it was so cheap. The room felt damp, and there was a slight smell of cigarette smoke in the air. There was nothing pleasant about this room, other than the fact that it was a roof over her head.

She sat down on the bed and picked up the landline. She dialed Gina's number and waited nervously. It went straight to voicemail. She sighed deeply as the wound in her heart grew a little deeper.

She picked up the small paper bag of medications that the doctor had given her and emptied it out onto the bed. She examined each of the plastic containers up close. The drugs all had long, complicated names she couldn't pronounce. They made her mind foggy.

She flicked open one of the containers and emptied a couple of the pills into her hand. She then put them in her mouth, and swallowed them dry.

Then she just sat there. Time seemed to stand still. It weighed on her with a crushing pressure. She felt like the walls of the room were closing in on her as darkness engulfed her mind.

Eventually she got up and wandered over to the mirror. She stared at her reflection for a moment. She looked so awful that even she couldn't deny it. She ran her hand through her hair and noticed that her roots were showing.

She walked over to the bed again and sat down once more. She just felt so alone, the emptiness she felt inside was almost a physical pain. She just wished she could rewind the clock, go back in time to a time when she was happy. Whenever that was. A long time ago, no doubt.

A memory came to her. She remembered the feeling of her father's warm arms wrapped tight around her, protecting her from the world and all in it. She could almost feel how good it was to be so safe, so loved, so wanted. How good it had been to feel as though there was a special place just for her!

She reached for the phone and dialed the motel's reception.

"Hi, do you have a number for a taxi?"

It had been years since she'd been stood in front of this house. She'd come here only once in her life, when she was fifteen. A friend and her had gotten drunk and somehow they had thought it would be a good idea to drive over here and confront her past face on. But she backed out at the last moment. They left without her even setting foot outside the car.

The house was really nice. It was a colonial style, well kept, freshly painted. A basketball hoop hung above the garage, and a grill stood in the front garden. It seemed like the kind of house that would be just as pleasant in summer as it would be in winter. It was warm, inviting, beautiful.

She noticed that the lights were on. She hesitated for a moment as an avalanche of doubts abruptly pierced through the fog of her mind.

As she placed her hand on the wooden gate her heart suddenly started beating really fast. She breathed in deeply and summoned up the resolve to keep going, but her body didn't move. She just stood there, frozen in fear.

All of a sudden a surge of determination swept over her, and she pushed the gate open. She walked down the path and pressed the doorbell. Adrenalin pumped through every vein in her body.

She waited for her father to answer.

Yeshua knew that the ordained time was upon him to meet his Destiny. The religious leaders were plotting against him; he knew this from the clearly distinguishable spies they had sent to the gatherings he had been speaking at recently. More than once he had been assailed by sly questions aimed to entrap him into saying something that could be used as an excuse to hand him over to the authorities. And he knew that though for now he was protected by the love of the people, it would not be long before their hearts turned against him too.

He breathed in deeply. It was almost time for him to face his biggest trial. He started to shake slightly. His hands were drenched with sweat.

He thought of Destiny. He thought of her beauty. He thought of how badly he wanted to be with her. He thought of how everything had been leading to this moment. And then calmness came over him.

He was going to win his bride.

Chapter Eleven

ALWAYS ON MY MIND

The woman who answered the door had a friendly face and a conservative but welcoming appearance. The smell of baking wafted out from inside the house when she opened the door, and the sound of a quiz show that was playing in the background filled the night air.

"Hello?" she said, a little quizzically.

Destiny suddenly felt horrendously awkward. She froze for a moment, which for some reason felt like an eternity. "May I speak to Ben, please?" she asked, her voice trembling a little as she did so.

"Yes, of course," the woman replied. She turned round to call back into the house. "Honey, someone's at the front door for you!"

Destiny could hear the sound of the television being turned off, and the noise of soft footsteps walking towards the door. She suddenly wondered if it was too late to run in the opposite direction. She felt faint. Pain and grief swelled up inside of her. It all felt too real for pleasure.

Suddenly he appeared at the door.

She was surprised at how very small he looked. And she barely recognized him. His hair had receded and deep lines had formed next to his eyes. Moreover, he seemed like he was from a different world than the one she had known him in so many years ago. She suddenly felt futile and illegitimate.

The woman quietly left, and Destiny just stared at him for a moment as the thought hit her that she was utterly intruding on the life he now had.

"Can I help you?" he asked. From the slightly guarded look on his face he clearly thought that she was a vagrant or there to ask for charity.

"Dad...it's me," she said, the words welling up from within her heart. "It's Destiny."

For a moment he looked at her in shock. Then he slowly got hold of himself.

"I'm...I'm intruding," she blurted out, feeling horrendously uncomfortable.

"No...no you're not," he exclaimed, still clearly stunned.

"I...I just wanted to see you," she said. Tears suddenly started to roll down her face. She was unable to speak another word, but her face said it all.

"Oh, Destiny," he said with a look of sheepish consternation as he stood there frigidly. He cast a brief glance inside. "I...em...I'm not sure that now is quite the right time..." His voice just trailed off into nothing.

Destiny felt like she had just been slapped in the face. For years she had known that her father was a coward. But to see him there, in person, so close and yet so far away, made her certain that the divide between them was more than a few feet. An anger suddenly welled up in her as she saw him for the first time as the man he truly was; fragile, scared and inept.

She felt herself losing control of herself. "Well, when is it going to be the right time, Dad, huh?!" she shrieked through her tears. "When? When we're both dead and buried, huh?! Is that when you want to do this?! Because I waited for you for years! I waited and I waited and I never stopped believing! And no matter what Mom told me I kept believing in you!"

"Destiny..." he said, trying to calm her down.

"Don't you dare *Destiny* me! Don't you dare ever say my name again! I'm dead to you! You want me gone; I'm gone! I'm done with you, and I don't ever want to see you again!" she cried. Then she turned her back to him and ran down the pathway without another word.

He called out her name, but it was too late.

Yeshua breathed in the cool air of the garden. He'd been lying there with his face to the ground for hours, as his friends lay asleep just a stone's throw away. His face was soaked with tears and sweat, and his whole body shook with grief as he contemplated the events he knew were about to unfold. His soul was overwhelmed with sorrow to the point where he felt like he was going to die from the burden of sadness that lay upon his heart. For though he knew that the time was coming when he would meet his Destiny, he also knew that the road that led there required a bloody and agonizing sacrifice.

He knew that his death would be brutal, for his enemies were vicious and their desire was for his total, public humiliation. He knew that the pain he was about to endure would be more than he could even fathom, and that his departure from this world would be horrendously slow and undignified.

He grasped at his tallit, which he had placed over his head. "Abba, Father, everything is possible for you! Take this cup from me!" he begged in anguish.

"Son, you know this is the only way you can receive your bride," the voice said.

"But all things are possible for you!" he cried out.

"This is the only way, Yeshua. If you wish to be joined with her in eternity you must pay the bridal price. This is the cost of loving her."

"But there must be another way, Father!" Yeshua pleaded.

"You know that she is your Destiny, Son," the voice said. "So will you give everything you are for her? Will you sacrifice your life for her love?"

Yeshua squeezed his eyes shut as tears poured out of them. He thought of his mother. He thought of his brothers. He thought of long, lazy afternoons in the wood shop, and of this land that he loved so much. The prospect of separation from them was almost too much to bare.

Yeshua pressed his head into the soil and screamed with all his might at the agony of his inner turmoil as he dug his fingers into the ground. The sound of his anguish seemed to echo in the cold night air.

Then suddenly he relaxed, his energy totally spent. He simply lay there for a while breathing in and out, deeply and slowly.

Eventually he lifted himself off the ground and knelt. He bowed his head.

"Father, if it is not possible for this cup to be taken away unless I drink it, may your will be done," he whispered into the night.

"You have what it takes, Son," the voice said in a warm and approving tone. "You are strong and you are bold, and you will win her heart. I am proud of you. Now get up; it is time!"

Yeshua smiled and stared up into the heavens. Then he stood to his feet. He walked over to his friends, and saw that they were still fast asleep. He reached out and shook them, "Are you still sleeping and resting?" he exclaimed. "Enough! The hour has come!"

His friends were slow to respond, and most of them just looked up at him bleary–eyed and confused.

Suddenly, Yeshua heard the sound of many footsteps coming towards him. He hastened in waking his friends up.

"Look," he exclaimed. "The Son of Man is delivered into the hands of sinners! Rise! Let us go! Here comes my betrayer!"

At that moment, Y'hudah, one of Yeshua's close friends, appeared with a small group of soldiers and some religious officials. Y'hudah knew this place well, as Yeshua and him had often socialized there. When Yeshua's friends saw that the group was carrying torches, lanterns and weapons, they quickly woke up.

When Y'hudah saw Yeshua he looked at him with a slight smirk.

"Teacher!" he exclaimed, and then reached over to kiss him. Yeshua knew in that moment that this was the kiss of a traitor.

Yeshua looked at him knowingly, straight in the eyes. "Do what you came for, friend," he challenged.

Y'hudah looked at him with a slight snarl, thrown by his candor. He threw a look at the soldiers. They abruptly stepped forward and seized Yeshua.

"By order of Rome, you are hereby under arrest," a soldier declared loudly.

As they bound him with rope Yeshua looked up at the heavens. He knew the end was nigh. His beautiful Destiny awaited.

Chapter Twelve

HERE COMES GOODBYE

Destiny browsed through the racks of alcohol that lined the liquor store wall. Jim Beam…Smirnoff…Baileys…ha, there was what she was looking for! Champagne, to celebrate never having to see or think of her father ever again! She smiled sardonically and made her way to the cashier.

It took Destiny hours to walk back to the motel. When she got back she turned on the bath tap. She cranked the tap to as hot as it could possibly go, and let the scorching water run over her hand for a moment. Then she lit some candles she'd picked up on the way home, and killed the lights. The soft glow of the candles and the sound of the water flowing immediately had a calming effect on her.

She wandered into the bedroom and pulled her clothes off, leaving them in a pile on the floor. She popped open the bottle of champagne, and returned to the bathroom with it.

As she got in the bath she could feel her whole body relax. She swigged some of the champagne, swallowing it as though it was water. The bathtub was almost full, so she reached over to turn the tap off, and then sunk back into the water.

She drank some more, this time knocking back the champagne in one go until she could no more. She could barely even taste it.

Time just stopped. A hazy numb glow took hold of her mind, as everything seemed to flow together. She watched the candles flickering and observed the colors in the flames.

She drank some more and then just lay there as her mind became increasingly anaesthetized.

She glanced over to the side of the tub, and saw a bottle of her pills there. She reached over and grabbed the bottle. She removed the lid, and as she did so a pill fell in the bathtub. She emptied some more into her hand. With the remainder of the champagne she swallowed them down.

Time passed. The haze grew stronger. Her whole body felt like it was floating. She could feel herself drifting into a peaceful darkness.

Once more she saw the bottle of pills propped up on the side of the bathtub. Barely conscious, she grabbed it, and emptied some of the contents into her mouth. She took some of the bath water in her hand and put it in her mouth, missing at first. Her eyes half closed, she chewed and swallowed, as drool ran down the side of her mouth.

She was so sleepy. So sleepy!

Slowly, her eyes closed.

Yeshua stood before Yosef Bar Kayafa, the high priest, weak, exhausted and emotionally drained. The religious leaders that packed the room were staring at him with such an intensity of hatred that he could feel it burning into his back. Yeshua had been standing before them for hours, shackled in chains, as false testimony after false testimony was given against him. The witnesses statements didn't even agree.

But Yeshua did not say a word. He refused to respond to such lies. He knew that the trial was a farce, and he already knew how it was going to end.

Yosef Bar Kayafa was visibly angry at his unassailable composure. Eventually his anger boiled over.

"Are you not going to answer?!" he demanded. "What is this testimony that these men are bringing against you?!"

Yeshua just stared at him.

"I charge you under oath by the living God, tell us if you are the Messiah, the Son of God!" he yelled.

"If I tell you," Yeshua replied calmly, "you will not believe me, and if I asked you, you would not answer. But from now on, the Son of Man will be seated at the right hand of the mighty God!"

"Are you then the Son of God?" Yosef Bar Kayafa demanded in a threatening tone.

"You say that I am," Yeshua answered.

Yosef Bar Kayafa went red with anger. He took his cloak between his hands and tore it dramatically.

"He has spoken blasphemy!" he yelled at the crowd. "Why do we need any more witnesses? We have heard it from his own lips! Look, now you have heard the blasphemy. What do you think?"

"He is worthy of death!" the crowd roared.

$$\infty\mathbb{O}\infty$$

Yeshua had been stripped almost entirely naked, and had been tightly bound to a post in a way that he was forced to stand with his back bent and his head bowed towards the ground.

He knew what was coming. He had heard many tales as a young boy of the Roman's brutal floggings, and his whole body was tense with the anticipation of the pain that was about to beset him.

Suddenly, The Tempter appeared before Yeshua.

"Yeshua, look what has happened to you, you're being humiliated! If you would just do as I ask this would all end in a moment," The Tempter exclaimed enticingly.

"I will have no part in your evil plans, Tempter!" Yeshua retorted.

He could hear the sound of the Roman dragging the flagrum across the ground towards him. The sound of the bone and the metal scraping across the stone floor made him feel like he was about to retch.

"She's not worth it! Why would you do this for someone who doesn't even know you exist?"

"Because I love her!" Yeshua replied.

"But she doesn't love you, does she?"

Yeshua didn't have time to respond before the Roman hit him with the first strike of the flagrum. Burning pain ripped through him and he screamed in agony. As the Roman pulled the flagrum back, skin was torn from his back. Blood started gushing down.

"She doesn't love you, does she?!" The Tempter screamed in his face. "She doesn't love you!"

Yeshua summoned up the little strength he had left in the midst of the pain. "Be gone!" he cried.

The Tempter snarled at him and disappeared. At that very moment the flagrum hit Yeshua again, this time exposing him down to the bone.

Yeshua was so weak and dehydrated that he could barely think. Cramps tortured his body. At times he felt barely conscious. The strain on his arms and shoulders was enormous, and the pain in his elbows was indescribable.

A few hours previously the soldiers had driven thick, hard nails through his wrists and feet, pinning him to a crudely made cross, and hanging him high for all to see. The position they had nailed him in made it extremely difficult to breathe, indeed almost impossible to take a full breath. He was forced to push up on his feet to get a gulp of air, and as his body weakened the pain in his feet and legs became unbearable. He was repeatedly forced to trade breathing for surrender to the pain and exhaustion.

At times he felt as though he was too tired to lift his body up far enough to get another breath, but then suffocation would start overcoming him and he would find the strength to fight some more. His heart was racing, pounding violently against his chest.

The pain was so unrelenting, so intense, that it almost had a flavor. It almost had a smell. It was all encompassing.

Dark, evil thoughts besieged Yeshua's mind. He could see The Tempter hovering before him as the weight of death bore down on him.

"You are going to fail, Yeshua! You are going to fail!" The Tempter proclaimed. "See, you wouldn't follow me, and now everyone is mocking you! And I mock you! I mock you!" he screeched with glee.

In that moment darkness poured into Yeshua's mind. All of a sudden he knew every pain, every burden, every dark and evil thought that Destiny had ever experienced. He could feel it all, he could see it all, he knew it all. The darkness and filth overwhelmed him.

Abruptly Yeshua cried out in agony, "My God, my God, why have you forsaken me?!"

The Tempter laughed raucously.

"I have won! I have won! Destiny will never be yours!" The Tempter declared.

With the little bit of energy he had left, Yeshua stared The Tempter defiantly in the eyes.

"It is finished!" he declared.

He looked up at the sky and cried out, "Father, into your hands I commit my spirit!"

Then Yeshua bowed his head and died.

As his final breath left his body The Tempter looked into the heavens. What he saw pierced him like a knife. Horror filled his face.

The Tempter let out a blood-curdling scream.

Chapter Thirteen

THE DANCE

When Destiny opened her eyes she was laying in the dark, face down on a hard, smooth floor. The coldness of the floor sent shivers the length of her naked body. She slowly tilted her head up to try to figure out where she was, and saw a figure standing above her. She could just see his outline from a faint light that came from beyond. Though she could tell from his posture that it was a man, his head was cloaked and so she could not see his face.

He slowly extended his hand to her, and she realized that he wanted to help her up. She lay there frozen for a moment, terrified of accepting his gesture. But then something inside of her compelled her to reach out, and so she allowed him to help her. She got to her feet, and stood before him.

She still could not see his face. Dark shadows obscured his features, and the thick linen that cloaked his head was wrapped around his entire body. Terror struck her heart as the sudden unfamiliarity of her surroundings and the shadows that surrounded her became very real to her.

The man lifted his hands to his cloak, and slowly removed it. As he did so she caught sight of his eyes. His eyes, his beautiful eyes, were full of such love, such compassion and such acceptance, that after just one moment of looking at them she was completely overwhelmed. Never before had she seen such purity, such beauty, such simplicity and yet such complexity. She was undone.

He cast off the fabric that had been covering his whole body. Immediately a bright light shone out of the white clothes he was wearing underneath, and indeed out of his entire being. As the fabric hit the floor it dissolved with a hiss. A dark and pungent vapor was released from it that almost instantly dissipated.

Destiny realized that she was no longer cold and that a pleasant warmth had infused her whole body. However she was also suddenly painfully aware of her nakedness. It was more than just an awareness of her physical appearance – she felt a sort of bare vulnerability she had never experienced before.

"Who are you?" she cried out.

"I am El Roi, the one who sees you!" the man said in a bold and commanding voice.

Destiny didn't know what to think. "Who are you?" she repeated.

"I am Yahweh-rapha, the one who heals you!"

She was still confused by his response, so she asked once more, "Who are you?"

"I am Yahweh-mekoddishkem, the one who sanctifies you!"

"What do you want with me?" she asked, deeply confused.

The man looked at her deeply in the eyes with a love and intensity that just took her breath away.

"Destiny, I have been in love with you since before you were even born," he declared. "I have given my life so that we can be together."

In that moment, though Destiny didn't know where she was, or indeed even how she had come to be there, she knew that this man truly loved her, and that she wanted to spend the rest of her life being loved by him.

"How…how do you know my name?" she asked in wonderment.

"It is engraved upon me," he replied with sincerity.

She dropped her head in shame.

"I am naked," she stated.

"Come with me, my love," he said with a smile, and held out his hand to her. As he did so she noticed that he had a profound wound running through his hand.

"You are wounded!" she exclaimed.

He smiled at her with deep affection. "I am complete," he said.

She didn't understand his words, but she took his hand none the less and followed him.

As they walked on she started noticing her surroundings. They were in a vast castle, with beautiful marble pillars, tall ceilings, and intricate chandeliers. Everything seemed to sparkle with an immaculate purity, and it glistened as the light shining out of the man passed it. She had never seen such opulence in her life, such beauty in every facet.

They reached a small room, surrounded with many ornate mirrors. As they entered it Destiny shuddered to see her nakedness reflected.

Then she saw that standing in the middle of the room was the most beautiful gown she had ever seen. It was white, with bellowing sleeves and a large train. It made her think of something that a medieval princess would wear.

He turned to look at her, with great excitement on his face.

"I have been waiting for many years to give this to you," he said.

Suddenly she broke into tears.

"I am not worthy of this dress!" she exclaimed, as she dropped her head once more.

Lovingly he took her face in his hands and lifted it until she was looking at him once more.

"You are worthy because of my love!" he said. As she saw the conviction in his eyes, the tough resolve and fire of his passion, she knew in that moment that his truth was the only truth.

He smiled gently. "Let me dress you," he said.

He carefully took the dress in his hands, and placed it over her head. As he pulled it down over her she could smell the sweet scent of lavender and rose. He gently laced the dress up. It fit her perfectly.

He led her over to one of the mirrors to see her reflection. When she did, she gasped. She barely recognized herself. She looked like a lady, or a princess, or a queen. She looked like a bride.

"I…I've never seen myself look like this!" she exclaimed.

"That's because you've never seen yourself through my eyes before. This is the way I've seen you every day of your life."

"Every day?" she asked with slight incredulity, her mind briefly flittering across some of her less than flattering moments.

"Every day," he stated with finality.

She looked at her reflection some more. Somehow, she felt like she was always supposed to be this way.

"And I have a surprise!" he continued with glee. He walked over to one of the walls and pressed on it, revealing a hidden closet. He took something out of it, and carefully hid it behind his back. He returned to her, and quickly revealed his surprise – two sparkling glass slippers sat on a purple and gold velvet cushion.

"These are for you!" he said with excitement.

Destiny giggled. "What, like Cinderella?" she exclaimed with slight unbelief.

He simply winked. In that moment she realized that he had a real sense of humor. She laughed in return. He got down on his knees and carefully slid the shoes onto her feet. They were just her size, and ever so comfortable. They sparkled and glimmered in a way that could only be described as magical.

He then returned to the closet and brought out a beautiful silver hairbrush. He brought it to her and, without a word, proceeded to lovingly brush her hair. Destiny felt humbled and overwhelmed that this amazing man would do such a tender thing for her. He kissed the back of her head when he was done.

"Come, my love, I have something more to show you," he whispered in her ear.

He led her to some tall double doors at the other side of the room. They were beautiful, made of sculpted gold and gemstones. He flung the doors open, and there beyond them she saw a grand ballroom, the like of which she'd never seen before. Tall pillars reached up to a beautiful vaulted ceiling, and a gold chandelier shone magnificently above. He led her into the center of the floor, and whirled her around. As he did so, music filled the room — a soft, slow, romantic piece.

He was an amazing dancer. His steps were so confident and bold that she didn't have to think – she just allowed herself to be carried along by him. He whirled her around, and her dress flowed and swept around the floor as he spun her around.

As she looked in his eyes a peace filled her heart. Finally, she could rest! Finally, she had found what she was looking for! Finally, she was fulfilled! She was loved and accepted in the most perfect of ways by a man who truly desired her!

As the music died down he bowed gallantly and kissed her hand. With a grin he then started leading her towards the far side of the room, towards yet another set of golden doors. As he flung the doors open she saw a vast theatre, with rich, burgundy, velvet drapes and plush burgundy and gold seats. A spotlight was shining on the center of the stage. A microphone had been placed in the middle of it.

"Will you sing for me?" he asked.

"I…I don't know," Destiny said, suddenly feeling very self-conscious.

"Please," he asked longingly.

Destiny knew she could not reasonably decline after all this man had done for her. So she approached the stage and climbed the stairs up to it. When she walked into the spotlight she could see him sat there, ready to listen. He was the only person in the audience, and yet she just knew that this was the most important crowd she had ever sung for.

"You know, I've been at every one of your performances," he said, smiling. "I've been at every show, at every competition."

"Why?" she asked with bewilderment.

"Because I love to hear you sing," he replied.

"I…I don't think I know a song that is worthy of you," she said.

He smiled once more. "I have placed a new song in you. If you just listen to your heart you will know it."

So she closed her eyes, and opened her mouth. And as she did so words started coming out of it, lyrics she had never heard before. She sung of his love for her, and of her love for him. She sung of how she loved being in his presence.

When she ended he applauded rapturously, and as he did she thought she heard the sound of a much vaster audience.

He ran up to the stage and joined her in the spotlight.

"I am so proud of you!" he exclaimed, and hugged her, swinging her round.

When he set her back on her feet she looked at him seriously. "Can I stay here with you forever?" she asked.

For a moment she saw a slight sadness in his eyes.

"I want you to choose to leave," he said, as he searched her face.

She suddenly felt terrified that she was going to lose him, and so she started to cry.

"I want you to go back to where you came from because I want you to use your beautiful voice to help restore other women, women like yourself," he explained tenderly.

"But I don't want to leave you!" she exclaimed.

"Destiny, I promise you this; I promise I will always be with you. There will not be a single moment in your life, a single breath that you breathe, when I will not be right there by your side, fighting for your love," he said.

"Then why? Why do I have to go back?" she cried.

"You have to go back because your world does not know who I really am. The women you see every day, they do not know who I am. I want you to go tell them the truth."

Destiny saw the pain in his eyes, the longing and the injustice. It hurt her heart.

"I...I want to help you, but I don't know how!" she exclaimed. "Why would they ever believe me if I told them about this place? I'm just one woman, and they don't care about anything I have to say!"

He lifted his hands up, and when he did so an intense light engulfed them. For a moment it eclipsed everything Destiny could see.

When the light subsided they were no longer in the theatre, but stood on a mountain by a cliff edge. In front of them was a wide valley, in which as far as the eye could see stretched a vast army.

Destiny looked out at the army. She saw that they were organized into regiments with military precision, and that each unit held a colorful banner. The banners depicted different symbols, with names emblazoned underneath such as HOPE, BREAKTHROUGH, UNITY, FAITH, CREATIVITY, PURITY. The soldiers were extremely tall, some of them two or three times the height of a man, and they shone from within with a pure white light. Their eyes looked like balls of fire, and their arms were strong. She knew they were warriors, but they looked unlike any warrior Destiny had ever known of before. She was awestruck.

He turned to look at Destiny. "This is my army," he said. "And now that you know me, they are your army too. They will fight for you. You have only to give the command."

"How do I do that?" Destiny asked, a little nervously.

"You do so in my name," he replied.

Destiny suddenly realized that she did not know his name.

"Then tell me what your name is," she demanded with boldness.

He looked at her dead on. "My name is Yeshua. But your people know me as Jesus."

Destiny gasped. Suddenly it all made sense. The marks on his wrist...the words he had spoken...this place. The realization of who he was washed over her.

It suddenly hit her that the marks on his hands were where he'd been crucified...for her. He had died...for her. Every nativity play, every stained glass window, every hymn she'd ever heard about him seemed so utterly inadequate to encapsulate who he was. She dropped to her knees, sobbing and penitent for all the ways that she had maligned and misrepresented him over the years.

"I'm so sorry! I'm so sorry Jesus! I never knew you! I never knew you!" she sobbed.

He reached down, and lifted her up.

"There are no yesterdays in my Kingdom!" he said, wiping the tears off of her face. "There are no tears of sorrow! There is no shame! There is only the beauty of my love for you, and the eternity we will spend together." He smiled a smile that was full of such purity and joy that Destiny knew in that moment that he had spoken truth. The power of his words washed over her, taking with them all her shame. She gasped, amazed at how light and free she suddenly felt.

He took her left hand, and placed upon it a beautiful ruby ring that was mounted on an intricate gold band. As he did so she noticed that the red of the ruby looked so much like the blood she could see in the gaping wounds in his hands.

"You are now my future bride, and as such you are royalty," he said with a smile. "All I have is yours. Every time you say my name, this army will go before you and behind you. They will cover your head, and make a way for your feet. Would you like to see how?"

She nodded vigorously.

He gestured towards the unit that was under the banner BREAKTHROUGH. "I command BREAKTHROUGH in the name of Jesus!" he exclaimed.

Instantly the soldiers under the BREAKTHROUGH banner held their swords up, roaring with a loud battle cry. Their banner lit up like a firework as red color and light exploded all around them. Thunder and lightening suddenly ripped through the sky above them. Destiny was in awe.

"Now you try!" he encouraged her.

In wonderment, she pointed towards the PURITY regiment.

"I command PURITY in the name of Jesus!" she cried out.

Instantly that unit held their swords up, roaring with a cry that had a ring to it. Their banner lit up like a firework as pure white light exploded in a vortex above their heads.

"Wow!" exclaimed Destiny. "Can I do it again?" she asked with the excitement of a little kid.

"Of course," he said with a chuckle.

"I command FAITH in the name of Jesus!" she cried out. Immediately the FAITH unit held their swords up, hollering with a cry that sounded like a lion's roar. Blue flares shot out of their banner as rain from the heavens started falling upon them.

This was the most awesome sight Destiny had ever seen. She felt so powerful, so strong. She was no longer afraid, as she had seen the mighty power that was going to accompany her wherever she went. She wanted others to feel as amazing as she felt, and she wanted others to see the incredible sights she was seeing.

She turned to face Jesus. "I will go," she said decisively.

"You have chosen well," he said.

He waved his hand, and a beautiful veil appeared in it. He placed the veil lovingly on her head, keeping her face uncovered.

"For a season we must dwell apart my love, simply as betrothed lovers," he said. "But a day will come when I will come for you, to bring you back to your true home. And then I will remove the veil, and we will be together forever," he said.

Then he brought the veil down over her face. Destiny was engulfed in darkness once more.

"Destiny!...Destiny!...Destiny!" a voice cried from far away. Slowly, Destiny opened her eyes. When she did her sight was fuzzy at first. As it came into focus she saw that Gina stood above her.

Destiny realized that she was lying on her side on the floor, and that vomit had formed a puddle by her mouth.

Gina looked frantic. When she saw that Destiny had opened her eyes she freaked out.

"Oh my God! Oh my God! Destiny?! Destiny can you hear me?!" she exclaimed.

Destiny suddenly realized that she felt weak and that her head was pounding. She nodded slowly.

"The ambulance is coming, Destiny! I'm so sorry, I didn't realize it was you calling me, and Rick didn't even tell me you'd been in hospital! I only found out today and then I had to track down your calls and then I convinced the guy to let me in because I saw your lights were on but you weren't answering the door! And then I found you and you gave me the biggest shock of my life! But it's going to be okay, it's all going to be okay, the ambulance is coming!"

Destiny lifted her hand, and placed it on her friends face. As she did so, she saw that the ring was still on her hand. She smiled.

She looked around the bathroom. The fresh light of early morning was shining through the window.

The night was over.

VANESSA FRANK grew up as a pastor's daughter, and gave her heart to the Lord at a young age. However as a teenager she faced several difficult circumstances, as a result of which she developed negative coping mechanisms such as alcohol and medication abuse, obsessive-compulsive disorder, anorexia and self-harming. Vanessa eventually realized that the only hope for recovery was to pursue healing through Christ with all her heart, all her soul, and all her might. She experienced deep emotional healing, and today remains free of these issues, living a life filled with joy, freedom and peace. She brings a message of hope, grace and renewal to young women facing such issues.

For further information see **www.vanessa-frank.com**

Acknowledgements

I thank the Holy Spirit for inspiring this book and for providing me with the revelation that first sparked this story. I thank God for giving me the skills and talents to bring this project to fruition. And I thank Yeshua for laying down his life so that I would have a message of hope to share.

Mummy and Daddy, thank you for championing this project and for believing that this was a story that needed to be told. Words fail to describe just how much your strength, support and prayer has meant to me. Many women's lives are going to be touched thanks to the support you have poured into this project, and I know you will receive your reward. I honor and value everything you have put into making this book a reality.

Libby Olsen and Leah James, you helped me to take this story to the next level. Thank you for reading my first draft and providing me with such excellent feedback.

Dr. Frank, thank you for assisting me with my medical research and for being so very patient with my rather macabre questions!

Grant Mahnken, you were a provision straight from Heaven and I give thanks to the one who sent you. Thank you for providing an exceptional proof reading service.

Lady Symphonia, thank you for the stunning artwork. There are very few people in the world who have an imagination like yours. I am in awe of your gifting, and so delighted to have been the recipient of it.

Amy Harris, I am so greatful for the beautiful author photographs. I've never felt as comfortable in front of a camera – you have a true gift. Thank you for creating some Italian romance deep in the heart of Tennessee.

Sarah Pharo, thank you for being such a wonderful blessing

whether it be as a graphic designer, a photographer's assistant, or simply as a friend. You were an absolute joy to work with.

Lisa Proctor, thank you for making me look so beautiful and for being such an encouragement and help throughout our photoshoot. When God told me to hire you He most definitely was recommending the very best!

Kelly Ritchie, it's always such a delight to sit in your chair. Thank you for making my hair so shiny and happy and pretty!

Mac Duggal, thank you for lending me two of the most beautiful dresses I have ever seen in my life. You have such a gift for bringing out the beauty in a woman's form, and I thank you for the generosity and kindness you showed in lending me these works of art.

Laura Gibson, wearing your creations made me experience a level of glamor that I believe every woman deserves. Thank you for lending me such beautiful jewelry.

Drew Hollowell, thank you for being such a wonderful representative of Yeshua, both on and off the screen. You were the perfect Cadbury's Milk Tray Man, and I know it was most certainly God who cast you.

Christine Poythress, thank you for terrifying me so much during our scene that I had no choice than to look scared! They say that acting is reacting, and when faced with such an excellent actress reacting isn't difficult to do at all.

Adam Sanner, I appreciate you being such a great sport. I'm sure you'll never watch Braveheart the same way again!

Matt Gantner, there are few people I could cast as a warrior angel, but you radiate light. Thank you for being willing to step in front of the camera and share that light with the world.

Justin Harvey, your involvement in this project was a divine appointment if I ever saw one. The strength of both your character and your skills was such an abundant blessing to this shoot.

Tony Wakefield, James Arnold, Steve Heydel, Tom Kovach and George Hurd, thank you for bringing the Sanhedrin to life, and for making those characters truly frightening.

Jon and Geri Bridston, thank you for supporting me in so many diverse ways, be it allowing me to turn your home into a film studio, dressing up in costume, providing incredible catering, or just being there to listen to me through the highs and the lows of this project. Thank you for being family to me.

Joel Banta, there aren't many DP's that would have had the guts to take on that shoot. The fact that you were so willing to embrace the challenge, and still find time to encourage me throughout it, speaks volumes to me of the destiny that God is building you up for. You are truly spirit breathed, and the atmosphere you create around you speaks to that. I await to watch your future unfold with excitement.

Jared Hicks, Zach Carlson, and Keith Perez, the industry needs more people like you! The incredible attitude, professionalism and focus you brought to such a gruelling shoot was outstanding, and was such a factor in its success. Thank you for bringing your 'A' game.

Ashley Burns, the costumes you designed and the wardrobe you put together were simply phenomenal. I am just blown away by your talent, and I know that a very bright future indeed awaits you. I thank God that I not only had the honor of working with you, but also of becoming your friend.

Char Braden and Neko Davis, I knew that you were the women for the job, and you proved me right a hundred times over. It blessed me all the way down to my toes to see the diligence and excellence that you brought to this shoot. You are true professionals.

Brooke Kallianos, thank you for the joy and light you brought to set. Your beauty is a blessing to all around you.

Alison Baker, you were an absolute answer to prayer. Your organizational skills, calmness, and incredible focus was such an wonderful help, and I valued every minute you were on set.

Dave Guyton, I feel like I should dedicate an entire page just to you. Thank you for your relentless commitment to seeing this project through, even in the midst of so many challenges. It's such a joy to work with someone who is such a visionary and an artisan, and who is totally willing to humor my obsession with Beauty and the Beast.

Patrick Lee Pond, Hunter Haines, and Megan Stokes thank you for being willing to do all that rotoscoping.

Jasmine Shinness, your voice is literally heavenly, and I thank the Lord for the way He ordained your involvement with this project.

To the many friends that have been a source of strength and healing in the last few years, who have supported me through countless prayers and encouragement, this work is a testimony to your love.

And to anyone I might have failed to mention – thank you for blessing me with your skills, talents and insight.